The Prince Mate

Alicia Simpson

Contents

The Begining Of It All

Natasha Lanning inhaled as she looked out of the carriage window. The castle was vastly spread out before her. It was a lot larger than she had ever imagined in her life. She had never been anywhere near a house of this magnitude. She couldn't believe that this was actually happening at this very moment. She thought back to when her mother told her about how this was all going to take place.

~Two Weeks Earlier~

"Natasha. I need you to pay very close attention to me" Her mother Victoria Lanning told her. There was a spike of irritation in her mothers voice she noted. Natasha turned away from her mirror and faced her mother fully.

"What is it mother" Natasha sighed heavily. Her mother was never her favorite person. She was a spiteful and mean person and she couldn't stand the woman. she barely even registered her as her mother at all. She heard her mother huff as she started to pace the floor in front of her.

"You are now a young woman. You should have been married long ago. No one wants to marry a stubborn, pig headed girl like you though. So, I've come up with a plan so that you might actually be able to get a man to even notice you. I have bought some new clothes for you. In about two weeks there will be a royal ball. You will be going to the ball and you will find a man before coming back who is willing to marry you. If you come back without a proposal or if you refuse to even go then I will marry you and your sister to whoever is willing to take you. " Her mother hadn't looked at her once as she told her all of this.

"You can't do that though! Bella is only thirteen!" Natasha stood up and glared at her mother. She couldn't believe her own ears. What kind of mother would send a child to get married? Then again she wasn't much of a mother in the first place.

"I can assure you that I very well can. So, it's up to you. Your sisters life is in your hands at the moment and it all depends on what you do as to what happens to Bella" Victoria told her.

Natasha stared unbelieving at the woman before her. The woman who had had two children held in her belly for nine months and then raised them for eighteen years altogether would give them away in the blink of an eye and to complete strangers. "So, what's in it for you" Natasha asked grinding her teeth. "What could possibly be in it for you" Natasha asked her.

"Well" her mother said as she sat on the edge of Natasha's mattress. "For one I get a house all to my own. Since your father is dead I don't really need to keep his kids around now do I? I'd also be getting money from whoever has the bad luck of marrying the two of you" Victoria smiled at her. "In all reality though, you might find your mate. It can't be that bad" her mother smiled at her.

"You really disgust me" Natasha spat her.

"That honestly doesn't offend me much. You've been a disgust to me since your birth. I thought little Bella would have been an improvement, but both of you are wretched little creatures" Victoria spat the words out at her. The venom in her voice and the hatred in her eyes was nothing compared to what Natasha was looking like right now. Natasha was livid. She had heard such things from Victoria all of her life, but she couldn't stand to hear anything about her sister. "You better be ready in two weeks" her mother told her as she quickly stormed out of the room.

~The Present~

Natasha exhaled quietly and closed her eyes. She had to find someone who would marry her and take her sister too. She couldn't let her mother stay anywhere near her sister for longer than necessary. She hope more than anything that she didn't find her mate here. Though, she really doubted that she would. She just didn't want to be tied down to a mate. They'd want to always be around her and what not. She just wanted a simple, rich man who, after two months of their wedding would pretty much forget about her. She felt a tear fall without her permission. She quickly wiped it away. She knew that she was going to have to lie to everyone in the castle. When she opened her eyes she saw a shooting star fly across the sky. She quickly wished that her lies would be believable and her sister would be safe until she could get her out of her mothers grasps. Suddenly the carriage came to a stop and her heart stopped also as the door was opened for her.

When Eyes Connect

Natasha was helped out of the carriage. She knew that what she was about to do wasn't right. She knew that she could get in a lot of trouble for this. She could be sent to prison or worse, put to death. She had heard many times that royalty didn't handle deceiving very well. She noticed that she was just standing there, frozen. She made herself put one foot in front of the other and walked down the path and to the castle entrance. 'Just breathe. Put one foot in front of the other. You've lied to your mother a million times and she's the toughest person to try and deceive. You're born to do this' she told herself in her head. She made her way to the front door where two guards stood watch. They had a long list between the two of them. "Name" the guard on the left asked her.

Natasha felt her throat constrict, making it hard for her to breathe. 'What if they knew who she was just by her name? what if they could tell that she was lying just by looking at her? What if they could smell that she was't royal? Was that even possible? What if none of this worked at all?' Thought after thought came crashing into her head at that moment. She had to answer and she had to answer now if this was going to work.

"Princess Natasha Lanning" She answered with as much strength in her voice as she was able. 'Your mother already set this up somehow. They'll have your name on the list. no one knows you here' she told herself. She watched nervously as the second guard looked for her name among the many on their list. He finally nodded to the other guard. The first guard smiled at her.

"Welcome" The first guard said as the two opened the doors for her. She stepped into the entrance with a sigh of relief. she couldn't believe that this was working so well. She took some deep breaths as the huge doors closed behind her and she was left to walk towards another pair of doors straight ahead of her. She looked down at her dress and smoothed it out a bit. She knew that she had the clothing of royalty, but would that be enough? She couldn't act like they did. She had to stop doubting herself so much. she could do this. She walked forward and opened the door and immediately heard music playing and chatter from all around the room. She closed the door behind herself and a short man asked her what her name was. She told him, unsure as to why he needed to know as well as the guards as to what her name was.

A trumpet blared as the man blew into the instrument. Everything became quiet all of a sudden. She became quite uncomfortable as everyone looked up the staircase and to her and the short man. "Natasha Lanning" he bellowed into the silence. She wasn't quite sure what to do next. The man glanced at her and gestured towards the stairs. She suddenly got what she was supposed to do. She started to make her way down the stairs and the music and chatter suddenly swelled across the room once again. She could tell that most of the people in here were royal werewolves. Some were royal humans. As she walked down the stairs, her gaze traveled around the room. Her eyes suddenly locked on another pair. She noticed how handsome he was and how graceful he was as he walked around the room.She was very attracted to this man ad she didn't know why. That was until her wolf started beaming from the inside. 'Mate' was the one word that it uttered and it echoed through out her mind. She couldn't have found her mate!

What she noticed as she studied him from head to toe was something she never could have expected. On his head sat a crown. He was the prince, he was her mate and he was walking her way.

Evading Fate

'He isn't walking towards you. Why would he? You're a nobody. Even if he does think you're royalty you wouldn't catch his eye. Though maybe he can tell that you are his mate? He probably still wouldn't care if he knew that you weren't a high class snob' Natasha told herself. she couldn't help but notice that he was still making his way towards her as she made her way down the stairs. She reached the last step and he was advancing quite fast. She noticed that he was barely paying attention to anyone else around him. Just her. He was only feet away when a woman interceded his path. It was a voluptuous blonde. She seemed to be late teens to early twenties and quite beautiful. for the first time the princes' eyes were off of her. She sighed in relief as the woman grabbed his hand and practically dragged him to the floor. She noticed him glance back at her. She saw something in his eyes that she had never seen before. Was it longing? She must be over thinking things. She quickly turned and disappeared in the crowd. Her wolf was growling at her to go and take her man away from the blondes wretched grasp. Her wolf wanted to come out and tear the obvious hair extensions out of her head before ending her life Natasha was in control though and continued to quickly walk away. She had to marry someone who was rich, but she would not marry the Prince or her mate. That was one sure way to get caught. He would surely want to know who her family was and he had enough power to actually figure it out if he really wanted to. Well, it's not like he'd ever want to marry her anyways. There were one too many pretty and rich girls out there to be worrying about a girl who looked like herself. She wasn't much to look at.

"Princess Natasha is it? What a beautiful name for such a beautiful woman such as yourself" a man who seemed to appear out of no where said as he took her hand in his and kissed the top of it. He was an older man. He seemed to be about fifty she was guessing. Natasha was only nineteen. She slowly and as politely as she could, extracted her hand from his.

"Yes. That's me. Who are you" she asked him. She hoped that she sounded like all the other royals. They always talked so uppity like they are better than everyone else and deserve words that the lower class doesn't. Like calling everyone darling or saying piche poche. They sounded pretty stupid to her, but maybe that's how society is.

"I'm Charles Sanders. Duke of Warrington." He smiled at her. She could tell he took pride in his title and expected her to have some sort of wonderful reaction. She tried her best to put on a face of admiration and surprise.

"Well, it's not every day that I meet a Duke" she told him. She could tell that he was pleased by her reaction. She could feel herself relax just slightly that her lie had worked. She knew she'd have a lot more lies to tell by the end of the night.

"Would you give me the honor of having the rest of this dance" he asked her. She suddenly felt panicked. Her mother had told her that she wouldn't have to dance. Just look pretty. Natasha couldn't dance to save her life. She had tried many times, but always looked terrible and almost every time tripped over some object or herself and fall on her face.

"I actually just want to get my bearings. It's such a beautiful place. I'd like to sit for a bit with a beverage and rest a bit. The ride here was pretty long"

Natasha made up the excuse as it came into her head. It sounded pretty terrible to her own ears, but he took it. He bowed gracefully.

"Maybe I'll receive a dance later then" he asked, raising an eyebrow as he stood back up straight. Natasha nodded and smiled. She politely excused herself. She walked to a table off in a corner. She didn't want to be noticed by anyone for a while. All of the lying was getting to her. She never liked to lie in the first place, but now she needed to. Her feet were already hurting a little bit from the wretched heels that her mother had thrown at her to wear. She grabbed a glass of what looked like some sort of champagne. She took a sip and let her eyes move across the room. The music had changed to another song and the beat of the song was more up beat. People swirled around the ball room. A shimmer caught her eye from across the room.

She glanced up to see the prince on the stand where there were two thrones sitting. He was above the crowd and looking around the room. Her eyes widened. He couldn't possibly be looking for her! She could sense him and she was sure that he could probably sense her too.His eyes fell on her and his face held a look of determination as he made his way down the stage and towards her. She knew he was in fact looking for her. What she didn't know was why. Yes, she was his mate, but she was a nobody. Though he didn't know that yet. She got up in a hurry and walked out as fast as she could without drawing much attention to herself. She glanced back once more to see the Prince's eyes on her as she walked out of the door and it closed behind her. She took a deep breath. She quickly walked down the hall. There had to be some place as to where she could hide until this all was over.

She had just turned the corer when she felt someone grab her arm and turn her around. She gasped in surprised and her eyes widened when she moved her gaze from the chest of the person in front of her to his face. It was the Prince and he was not happy.

Prince Charming

Natasha felt her breath hitch I her throat as she continued to stare into the Prince's eyes. They were smoldering with something that wasn't exactly anger. Maybe it was anger and confusion? "Why are you avoiding me" he asked. There was definitely confusion in his voice. She wasn't exactly sure as to how she was supposed to answer his question. She decided to try and pull her arm away from him to buy her some time to think about how to answer. His grip stayed firm. "Answer me" he said softly. He seemed more confused than angry now.

"I just don't like to converse with Prince's" Natasha told him. It wasn't a lie either. she'd rather be anywhere else at the moment than talking to the prince.

"But you don't mind talking to a Duke" he asked her with a raised eyebrow. She could tell that he didn't believe her like she had thought that he would have.

"Well, he came up to me in started to talk with me. It would be quite rude and unlady like for me to not respond. Would it not" she asked him. She raised an eyebrow back at him to mimic him. "Besides. I'm talking to you at the moment. Am I not? This is no different than how it was with the Duke"

Natasha told him. "Though I don't see why it should matter to you. You seemed to be just fine with the woman you danced with before. You should keep your attention on those who seem to be interested in the attention and not on those who aren't. Now if you would excuse me. I have to be finding a restroom" she told him and removed his had from her arm and turned on her heels and started to walk away from him.

"The closest washroom is right there" she heard the Prince say. When she turned around she looked at the door he was pointing at. She nodded her head before walking to the door and sighed at her mistake. Of course they'd have a fancy name for a bathroom. A wash room. She'd have to remember that.

"Thank you" she said quietly. She curtsied quickly once she remembered her manners and walked into the room. It was rather nice in here. She sat on a cushioned settee' while she waited for it to be the appropriate time for her to leave once again. She never wanted to exit the safe haven of the washroom ever again wit the vulture prince lurking around. That made him sound creepy. He of course wasn't. He was actually quite handsome and sophisticated, but he did seem a little egotistic. Like with her not immediately talking to him. It's not like it was a rule for every eligible girl to converse with him. She rolled her eyes as she straightened her dress and walked back out of the room with the Prince no where to be found.

She sighed in relief as she walked into the ballroom. She didn't see the Prince when she glanced round. She smiled to herself. Maybe he had been swept off his feet by some princess and he was not even thinking about her anymore. Now that was a rather fine idea in her mind. She was heading back to her seat as the songs changed and she was gazing around the room when she bumped into a solid chest. She almost lost her balance when she felt an arm around her waist and a hand on her arm. She felt sparks tingle up and down her arms making her heart skip a beat or two. She gasped and her eyes flickered up to the face of her savior. "May I have this dance" the Prince asked her with the most charming smile on his face. Prince charming indeed.

Hoping To Be Forgotten

Natasha was trying to figure out a excuse to get out of this dance with him as he pulled her to her feet. The sparks running from her arm all the way through out her body wasn't helping her brain to think though. She was about to tell him that she was just a terrible dancer, but the Duke of Warrington suddenly showed up. "I would dance with you, but I already promised my first dance to the Duke" she said extracting her hand from the Prince's. She felt the Prince's breath on her neck.

"He may get your first, but I'll get your last" he promised her. With that, he was gone. She took a deep breath and put her hand in the Duke's. For some reason, just the feel of his hand on her arm just felt so right. So unlike her hand touching the Duke's. In fact, the Duke was just creepy in all honesty. She just couldn't be stuck with someone like the prince. Why would he want her sister to be part of a package with her? Well, why would anyone want to have her sister be part of the package? She realized that no one would. This was pretty much a lost cause. She bit her lip and figured that she was just going to disappear after this song. She couldn't stay and lie anymore for nothing. She came back to the present to see herself gracefully dancing across the room with the Duke. This couldn't be her right? Then she thought about it and realized that she was just following him. It wasn't as hard as she and thought that it would have been.

Natasha sighed in relief when the song was over. She retracted her hand from his and curtsied as he bowed. "It was a very lovely dance" he told her. Natasha smiled and replied with the same. She looked around for the closest exit. There was a side door that looked like it went out to the garden. She made her way over to the door. The entire time her wolf was howling and telling her not to leave their mate. She blocked her wolf out as much as possible. She made it to the garden door and got outside. She saw the moon high in the sky with stars sprinkling out across the sky. It was pure beauty. She shook her head in disappointment. This night was nothing like she expected. She never expected to meet her mate or not find a husband. 'Oh, well. Things happen' she told herself. She had to get back home and try to reason with her mother. Telling her that she could get her as much money as she wanted, but it would just take a bit of time. She'd get three jobs if she had to and she could sell her off if she wanted. She just didn't want anything to happen to Bella.

She took off her shoes. She knew that she'd ruin the lovely dress by shifting, but she didn't care. She just knew that she could get to the train a lot faster if she was in her wolf form. She transformed and then just started running. She heard someone calling her name and somehow she knew that it was the Prince. It pushed her to go faster. She suddenly heard a howl in the darkness and her heart almost stopped. That couldn't be the Prince, could it? Her wolf answered though. She tried to quiet her and went faster. She could hear something coming behind her though and it was coming fast. Him being of royal blood made it so that he was very fast. Besides he was a male and males were more common to be faster. She dodged to the left to try to get him to slow down a bit, but he only seemed to be gaining on her. Before she knew it, he was right behind her. She growled at him when he nipped at her tail.

Her heart was thumping in her chest there was no way that she could get away from him at this point. She suddenly felt a force pushing her into the ground. She had slid a ways before coming to a stop. She felt his presence standing over her. He was growling and there was a rumble in his chest. She had never been afraid of anyone, but she felt a tinge of fear because of him. He moved so he was off of her and was pacing not to far away. She slowly stood up and moved so she could watch him. She didn't know why he couldn't just let her go? He suddenly was a human. He shifted? why would he shift when he knew what was going to happen. She had caught a glimpse of his naked self, before quickly looking away. She growled lowly when he started coming towards her. "Don't growl at me" he told her. She slowly started to back away as he advanced towards her. "Stop backing away" he said, becoming frustrated. She suddenly stopped. Her wolf whimpered. Why was her wolf so weak? "Why don't you want me" he whispered. He got down on his knees before her. His voice sounded so sad and broken. She looked at his face. Just his face.

She closed her eyes and shifted before quickly moving so she was covering everything. She sat on the ground and pulled her knees up to her chest, wrapped her arms around her legs, and leaned her chin on her knees. "You don't really know me and if you did, you wouldn't want to be with me" she whispered.

Starting To Accept Fate

I'm sorry about any spelling errors. My old keyboard would leave out the letter "n" a lot and I have a new keyboard that doesn't do that. I hope you enjoy the story so far! :)

~~~~~~

Natasha could tell that he wanted to move closer, but he didn't. She stared at the ground, too afraid to see the hurt in his eyes. Her wolf was howling in pain from the mere glimpse she had seen just a few seconds ago. "You're my mate. Why would I not want to be with you" Emen asked her. She could hear the pleading in his voice and it caused a stomach wrenching reaction from her wolf. She couldn't tell him the truth. That she was from a poor family. The whole mate thing would be nothing after that. No one wanted to marry someone who wasn't of the same financial group as themselves.

"Look. I come with a lot of baggage. I have a little sister who I just can't possibly leave. I'd have to bring her and who would want-" she was stopped by a hand on her chin. Just the feel of the tips of his fingers sent sparks across her skin.
~~~~~~

"I would. I'd love your sister as if she were my own. If you want to bring her, then bring her here! I don't want anything to stop you from being with me. Absolutely nothing" the Prince told her and let go of her chin.

"I don't even know your name!" She exclaimed. She was getting desperate. She couldn't tell him the truth. He could have her put to death. What would happen to her sister if that were to happen? she shuddered at the thought.

"My name is Emen" he told her. His voice sounded so helpless. Like he wanted her to stay so bad, but he could see that she wasn't wanting to stay all that much.

"Prince Emen" Natasha whispered to herself. It was a lovely name for such a lovely man. She just wished that she could tell him the truth. She would if she knew one hundred percent that he wouldn't react badly to knowing the truth about her.

"Emen. Just Emen to you" Emen told her. She closed her eyes and sighed.

"I'm sorry, but it's not right for me to just call you by your first name" she told him.

"You're my mate! You have more right than anyone else to call me by my first name" he exclaimed. He stood up and started pacing. Seeming to not care that he was in the nude at the moment. "I don't see why you don't want to be with me. My wolf and I are going crazy for the both of you" emen cried out. It echoed across the night. His sorrow and pain. She couldn't stand him being in so much pain.

"I want to be with you more than anything, but you don't know the real me. What you saw back at the ball? That wasn't me. I'm not this fancy girl that you're picturing right now" Natasha told him. She felt herself breaking down. She couldn't stand to know that she had hurt him so bad.

"All I know is, is that you're my mate" he said and stopped pacing. He kneeled down in front of her once more and took her chin in his palm so she was now staring into his eyes. "My heart is aching for you so much right now that it hurts" he told her. She could see the truth in his eyes.

"Nobody else will accept me like you might though. I'm sure your family won't" Natasha whispered. Her resolve was breaking. She couldn't just leave him now.

"It doesn't matter. They can't control who is my mate and who is not. It doesn't matter to me what anyone else thinks. You mean the world to me and that's all that I need to know" Emen told her. He was smiling now. She felt better knowing that he wasn't hurting so much.

"Look. I think we should probably go back. Everybody will be looking for you. They probably already have a search party out for you" Natasha told him. Emen shrugged as he stood up.

"At least I can go back and announce that I have found my mate" he smiled at her.

"Yeah" she said and paused for a moment. She still wasn't sure how she felt about this at all. "I just need some clothes when we get back" she told him. She heard him laugh before he shifted into his wolf form. She shifted too and looked over at him. He was beautiful in animal form too. She smiled, which probably looked pretty weird in dog form. The two of them made it back to the castle. They went through a different door and up some stairs. They made it to a different room, which she soon realized was his room. She almost walked back out, but he nudged her in. He closed the door before shifting back to human as he went into his closet. He changed quickly before coming back out. "Well, I need to look for some clothes for you" he smiled at her. He scratched between her ears before leaving the room and shutting her in. The door re-opened and a girl came in with a beautiful gown.

"You can shift now miss" the girl told her. She did after a moment of hesitating. She was helped into the gown and given the shoes that she had, had on earlier. She slipped them on before standing up. "He is waiting for you down stairs miss" the girl informed her. She thanked her before going downstairs to see the Prince at the entrance of the ballroom. He held out his elbow for her to put her arm through. She did so and they walked down the huge stairs together. They made their way up to the stage that Emen had been on earlier. He motioned to the short man at the top of the stairs and the man blew his horn.

"Prince Emen has something he'd like to announce to everyone" the man shouted across the room.

Every eye in the room went to the two of them, standing on the stage. "Thank you. So, as everyone knows. I haven't found my mate for all these years. We have all been hoping that that day would come. Well" he said grinning as he held her hand in his. "I have found her. This is my mate. Princess Natasha" he announced. There was clapping through out the room. She held her breath as the words he just said rolled around in her head. "Princess. Princess. Princess" He'd never want to know that she wasn't one. She looked around the crowd at all of the faces and her eyes landed on two specific faces. They held a look of surprise. They were the queen and king.

Meeting The King and Queen

N atasha felt her throat constrict because of stress, making it hard for her to breathe. She was standing here, lying to every royal person in this room, her mate, and his parents who are the rulers over everyone else. Her grip on his hand tightened. So much that he glanced over at her. His head dipped so his mouth was closer to her ear. "Are you alright. You're looking a little flushed" he asked her concerned.

"Fine" she responded and put on a fake smile. So many things were running through her head right now. Like what if his parents didn't like her? What if Emen found out the truth? What if his parents found out the truth? What was going to happen with her sister? She closed her eyes for a moment. She just wished that she was back at home, even though that would mean that she'd be with her wretched mother. She reopened her eyes as the clapping died down. She noticed that Emen was looking at her. Well, it didn't seem like he believed that lie. She also noticed that the King and Queen were on their way up the stage. The Queen made it to them first.

"Oh this is a wonderful, magnificent day! We all really were starting to wonder if my sweet son would find a mate at all and here you are. Such a beautiful young girl. A Princess to match. We will just have to meet your family as well. Won't we? Did they come with you" The Queen asked her with a huge smile on her face. She could tell that his mother was very excited to know that her son has finally found a mate. The Queen seemed like a very sweet woman.

"No. They didn't come with me. My mother is at home with my sister. My father is dead" Natasha told them and tried to not make it seem like her fathers death was all that big of a deal.

"Oh. That is just terrible. I'm sure we'll meet you mother and sister soon though. I'm sure you'll be sticking around so we'll have to have a one on one chat very soon. Okay" the Queen asked her.

"Of course your majesty" Natasha smiled back and curtsied.

"Nope. None of that. You are my sons mate. You have no need to curtsy or call me majesty. Linda will do" Linda smiled at her. "Oh! I almost forgot. This is my husband John" she smiled at him. You could see the adoration in her eyes. The King looked at her and gave her a soft smile.

"It is a pleasure meeting you Natasha. I look forward to getting to know you" he told her. "You may call me John as well" he told her after a small nudge from his wife. He seemed a little less enthusiastic, but very kind.

"It is really nice to meet the both of you" Natasha told them sincerely.

"Well, we best be going. We should give the two of you some space" Linda said dragging John away.

"Your parents are very lovely people. Your mother is very energetic and sweet" Natasha commented as they walked away. She turned to Emen who was looking at her. "What" she asked him.

"You didn't tell me that you had a mother. I thought that when you said that you'd have to bring your sister that the two of you didn't have anyone else" emen told her confused.

"Well, maybe you shouldn't just assume things. I never wanted my mother to come, because she is a terrible woman. That's why I need to bring my sister. So that she isn't in my mothers hold" Natasha told him and kept her eyes averted from him. She felt his hand under his chin and felt her head being tilted back so that her eyes would meet his.

"Did she ever hurt you" he asked her. His voice sounded so cold. This was the most serious she had ever heard him since she met him.

"No. Not physically anyway" she told him with a shrug, like it was no big deal.

"But she's hurt you other ways" he asked her, still serious.

"I mean. Saying rude things about me or my sister and just put down sort of things. Nothing too big. I deal with it, but I don't want Bella to have that happen to her" Natasha told him. She didn't bring up the fact that her mother was going to sell her sister and herself if she couldn't find someone to marry her and take in her sister.

"You better hope that I don't see your mother. I will tell her how I feel about her" Emen told her. She could see some rage building in his eyes. She was glad that she hadn't told him anything more, because she was sure that he'd be really angry then.

"I never want you to meet my mom anyways. Bella is a little sweet heart though" Natasha smiled at the thought of her sister.

"How old is she" he asked with a smile at the change of subjects.

"She's thirteen. Such a beautiful young girl too" Natasha sighed to herself as she imagined her sister standing there with them.

"We can leave to go get her tomorrow if you'd like" Emen told her. She couldn't let him see their home. He would figure everything out.

"I think it would be best if I were to just go"Natasha told him.

"And let something happen to you? I don't think so" Emen told her.

Natasha sighed to herself and just nodded her agreement. She'd figure something out. If anything she could just tell him on the way the entire truth. Emen pulled on her hand as he walked. She didn't know where he was going until they reached the middle of the dance floor. She felt one hand go to her waist as the other stayed in her hand. She put her other hand on his shoulder and they gracefully glided across the ballroom. She just stared at his face the entire time they danced with a huge smile on her face. This is one of the first times that she was truly happy in a very long time. The song ended earlier than she wanted it to. "I told you I'd get the last dance with you" Emen whispered in her ear before kissing her cheek. She felt a blush rise and swell over her cheeks. He started walking and she followed. Everyone was leaving and she assumed that she'd be staying in some guest house or something. She noticed that Linda and John had appeared out of no where.

"So, you looked like such a lovely couple out on the dance floor" Linda smiled at her.

"Thank you" Natasha and Emen said at the very same time.

"So, I believe that Emen will be showing you where you will be staying" John told her.

"I want to have the chat tomorrow with you Natasha" Linda told her.

"Mother. We'll be going to go get her sister tomorrow so that she can stay with us" Emen cut in.

"It will only take but a moment Emen" Linda told her. Natasha could tell that Emen didn't like the idea of his mother side tracking her, but she didn't want to be rude. Especially to the Queen.

"So I will see you both tomorrow then. Good night" Natasha told them. They all said their good nights and Emen showed her where her room would be. Which was up two flights of stairs and down a hall.

"So, my room is right across from yours. There should be something to sleep in, in your room. If you'd like a bath or something, there is a bathroom in there. Other than that, I think I'll see you in the morning" Emen told her with a smile.

Natasha smiled back at him. "Thank you so very much. I'll see you tomorrow then" Natasha told him. She smiled one last time at him before turning to the door. She had just put her hand on the handle before she was turned back around and pushed against the door. She looked up to see Emen's body pressing against hers. His head was leaning closer and closer to her as his one hand found her waist and the other hand found the back of her neck. She watched as his head dipped down and she closed her eyes as she felt his lips softly brush against hers. Suddenly the feeling of his lips and body were gone. She opened her eyes to see him opening his own door.

"Good night" Emen winked at her before going into his room and closing the door. Her mouth was slightly open as she stared at his door. That was it? That was the kind of kisses he gave out? She went into her room and closed the door, leaning back against it. She sighed and closed her eyes. That was her first kiss and even though it was short and barely even a kiss, it was perfect.

Nightmares

~ ~~A/N~~~

So, I was hoping that some people could help me by commenting and telling me what you either like or dislike. I'm really thankful for who ever is still reading. :)

~~~

Natasha had taken a bath, changed into a night gown that was left in the room for her and then fell asleep. She dreamed of Emen.

Dream

Natasha was sitting on Emen's lap, playing with his hair. They were both looking into each others eyes, smiling. They began laughing about something. He cupped her face in his hands and kissed her lightly on the lips. She was excited about something, but she couldn't tell what. The carriage came to a sudden stop and they both smiled at each other. "We're here" Natasha said really excited. She got out before Emen could open the door for her. She was bouncing on the balls of her feet as she waited for his reaction. Emen got out of the carriage and smiled at her before turning to a house.
~~~

It was her house. His smile suddenly disappeared. He turned his eyes on her. There was confusion and anger in his eyes.

"How could you lie to me? Maybe it's because you know that I'd never like someone like you. I can't believe I wasted my time on you! You are such a waste of space. A good for nothing peasant" Emen shouted at her. He gripped her arm and started to drag her back into the carriage. Natasha was crying her eyes out.

"I'm sorry! Please forgive me. I never wanted to hurt you! Please Emen. Please" Natasha begged him. She felt her heart breaking.

"You have no right to use my name" he spat at her. Natasha turned her head and saw her mother and Bella outside. There was a man there too. There were tears going down Bella's face.

"How could you do this to me Natasha? I loved you! You let me down. You are a worthless sister" Bella cried out as the man took hold of her arm. Her mother had a sick smile on her face as she looked inside of a bag that the man had given her. Money more than likely.

"Bella! I tried. I'm sorry! I tried" Natasha cried out. She tried wrenching herself free from the Prince, but he wouldn't let her go. "Bella! Bella!" Natasha screamed as she was dragged towards the carriage and the man dragged Bella into another carriage. Natasha could barely see through her tears. "Let her go! She's just a little girl! I'll find you Bella" Natasha cried out as she was shoved into the carriage. The Prince climbed in after her. The dream switched to a stone room. It was freezing inside the room. The door opened, blinding her for a few minutes. A man grabbed her shackled wrists and dragged her to her feet. She silently followed the man in tattered clothing. No shoes on her feet. She was taken outside.

There was a huge crowd gathered. As the man led her up wooden steps, she noticed faces. Her mother, Prince Emen, Queen Linda, King John, and even Bella with that man. Natasha stared at each one. Anger was all that she saw from all of them. She made it to the top of the plat form and realized what they were going to do! She was brought to the middle and a noose was brought down and put around her neck. "Please don't do this to me! I don't deserve it! Please" Natasha cried out. She had thought that the tears would have been dried up by now, but they started to flow once more. She watched as the people she recognized came to stand in front of her. First her mother stood there.

"You do deserve this. You are a wretched creature that was a mistake since you were born. This is what happens to worthless things like you" her mother told her. Her chest was starting to ache from the pain she was going through. Her sister Bella came next. There were purple marks marring her little sisters skin. The man was abusing her. He was grabbing her shoulder at this very moment. Through the sadness and worry, she felt angry still towards the man.

"How dare you harm her! you will regret what you have done" Natasha screamed at him.

"It's your fault Natasha. If you had just gotten married and brought me home with you guys, then I wouldn't have been taken away by him. He wouldn't hurt me. It's all your fault. How could you do this to me? Falling for a Prince. He wouldn't love you enough to stay with you once he knew you were poor. Why couldn't you just marry a nobody. Someone who wouldn't care. Then I wouldn't be in this. I wouldn't be getting hurt. I hate you" Bella screamed at her. Natasha felt her eyes become blurry as they stepped away. She was full out crying now. Her sobs wracking her body. The only thing making it so she'd stand was the rope around her neck. The King and Queen showed up next.

"I'm so sorry" Natasha choked out.

"You lied to us and our son. You are getting what you deserve. We just wish that we could have seen you for who you truly are before our son touched your filthy self"The Queen told her. The two walked away without looking at her again. Emen was standing in front of her now and she couldn't even see his face through her tears.

"You lied to me. You lied to my family. You pretended to be royal when you aren't anything, but a filthy poor nothing. I feel nothing for you at this moment and can't wait for your existence to be demolished. You deserve what you're getting" Emen told her. There was hurt and anger in his voice. She choked out a sob as he walked away from her.

"Please! I'm sorry. I've been trying to do what's right. I've tried! It wasn't the right thing to do though! I'm sorry! Please, forgive me. Let me show you that I am not who you think I am! Please! Anyone? You can't do this to me. I love you all so much" Natasha cried out.

"It's much too late for that" She heard Emen's voice call out right before the floor beneath her feet disappeared and she fell and-

Dream over

She jerked awake right before her death happened. She was being shaken by the Prince. There were tears streaming down her face as she looked at him. "Natasha. Are you okay" Emen asked her. He stopped shaking her when he noticed that she was awake.

"You don't hate me" she whispered. Her eyes were wide and frightened. Well, as wide as they could be with tears coming out of them. Emen looked at her with surprise and concern.

"No Baby. I'd never hate you" he whispered as he wrapped his arms around her and wiped the tears away with one hand. "What were you dreaming about" Emen asked her, worried.

"Just please forget about it" she whispered as she clung to him for dear life. 'Because I will never be able to' she thought in her head as she closed her eyes and breathed in his scent. She hoped that her nightmare never came true. Well, she was soon going to find out.

A Step In The Right Direction

Natasha woke up the next morning and found a dress in the bathroom. It was a casual, but very elegant dress. She put it on and a pair of shoes that must have been left there last night. She decided not to wake up Emen and went to go find the dining room. She walked all the way to the first floor, because she was guessing this floor would be where it's at. She decided to ask the first person that walked by. It was a girl around her age in a maid uniform. "Excuse me. Could you possibly help me find the dining room" she asked her. The girl was very beautiful.

"Here, I'll show you" the maid told her. She didn't seem too happy about showing her or even talking to her. The girl who looked around her age showed her to the dining room before leaving with a huff. Well, someone didn't seem to like her very much. Natasha walked into the Dining Room and paused with wide eyes at what she saw. There were at least 60 werewolves in the room at that very moment and she knew none of them. All of their eyes went to her and their conversations stopped.

"Well, look who it is" a red head said with a goofy grin on his face. He seemed to be slightly younger than herself. "So, you'll be the new Luna after you and Emen marry and you go through the ceremony right" he asked her. Natasha looked at him and shrugged.

"I mean I guess that's how it would work right" she asked him. She should probably know the answer, but she still wasn't sure if she was just going to end up leaving or not.

"Well, it's a pleasure to meet you. I'm Sam. It's really nice to meet you" Sam said as he held out his hand for her to shake. She walked along the side of the table to where he was sitting and shook his hand.

"The pleasure is all mine. I'm Natasha" she told him. All of a sudden it was a mad house. Everyone wanted their soon-to-be Luna to know their names and shake her hand as well. Sam stood in front of her and pushed her into the corner and pushed some of the guys that were getting too close to her and getting too rough.

"You all need to calm down right now" Sam yelled at them. Some did, but others continued. Suddenly one of the aggressive werewolves was thrown off to the side and another throne at the table, making food go everywhere. There was a menacing growl coming from Emen. The rest of the aggressive males backed away quite fast. Same moved slightly so he wasn't blocking Natasha from Emen, but still ready to help keep other werewolves away. Emen grabbed her and pulled her into his arms. He checked to make sure she was okay.

"Did anyone touch you" emen asked her. He was being dead serious.

"No. I just shook Sam's' hand and then everybody went crazy. I mean I guess they were just excited about meeting their future Luna I guess" Natasha tried to explain. She didn't want them to get into any trouble.

Well, Sam is the future Beta so I'm fine with that. He's also my best friend" Emen smiled at Sam. "Thanks for protecting her" Emen said putting his hand on Sam's shoulder. Sam just nodded as a reply and looked at the werewolves around the room. "If I see this happen again then whoever is participating in the bothering of my mate will be severely punished.. Is that understood" Emen asked. There were immediate "yes" answers throughout the entire room before it fell silent again. Emen turned to Natasha as everyone sat in their seats and started eating and their conversations again. "Why didn't you come get me when you wanted to come down here" Emen asked her confused and a little hurt. Natasha sighed and tried her hardest not to roll her eyes. This is exactly what she was worried about happening. Having a mate and having them watch her every move pretty much.

"I thought you could use the sleep with me waking you up in the middle of the night. I was just going to find something to eat real quick before going to have that talk with your mother so that we can go get my sister" Natasha shrugged.

"Well, you're not eating out here today. Lets go to the kitchen and we can eat there" Emen told her. He took her hand and directed her towards the kitchen. She looked back to see Sam wave at her and smiled. She liked Sam already. When they got into the kitchen they sat down on a couple of stools that were at a granite counter. "What would you like to eat" Emen asked.

"Anything is fine with me" Natasha shrugged. She really didn't care, because she wasn't all that hungry at the moment.

"Okay. Thomas can you make two omelets" Emen asked a big guy at the stove.

"Well, my father used to tell us when he was still alive to never trust a skinny cook" Natasha said quietly. She blushed when Thomas bellowed out a laugh. "I'm sorry I didn't even mean to say that out loud" Natasha apologized quickly.

"I like this girl" Thomas told emen and gave her a friendly wink before turning back to the stove. Natasha smiled. So many people were friendly here. She frowned, but what if she had to leave if she told Emen the truth? Well, she still had some time to figure out if she wanted to tell him or not. She bit her lip as Thomas laid the plates in front of them and gave them forks with a drink.

"I like her too" Emen said staring at her. Natasha averted her eyes from him and horridly ate as fast as she could, burning her mouth on the hot eggs as she put them in her mouth. She swallowed before looking at him.

"I do believe it is time to have that talk with your mother" Natasha stated. emen was already done.

"Alright. Thanks Thomas" emen called over his shoulder as he took her hand in his once again and brought her to a room with a couple couches and comfy looking chairs. Linda was already there, sipping a drink out of a tea cup. "I'll come back in an hour on the dot so we can head out" Emen told. Natasha nodded and watched him leave and shut the door.

"Natasha dear! Please sit down. I am quite excited to hear about you. You just spark my interest so much for some reason" Linda told her. Natasha smiled at her. This woman was the kind of mother figure that she wished her actual mother was like.

"I don't really know what you'd like to hear about me. I'm not really all that exciting" Natasha admitted to her as she sat down on a comfy chair.

"Don't be so modest" the queen told her with a smile. "Tell me about your home, family, things you're used to" She smiled at her. Natasha watched the queen. she seemed so interested in learning about her soon to be daughter-in-law. She was just a kind hearted woman from what she could tell. She wasn't too sure she could actually lie to her. She thought that she should start with not lying and at a safe point.

"Well, my sister is thirteen. She is the most adorable girl that I've ever seen. She's so intelligent and kind hearted" Natasha smiled as she thought about her sister. "She loves walking around and exploring things" she added.

"It seems that she has many of your qualities" Linda told her. Natasha looked over at her and her heart ache. She was nothing like her little sister. She was lying to all of these people and pretending to be something that she wasn't.

"Look your majesty" Natasha said as she looked at her hands and played with the edge of her dress sleeves. "I'm not who all of you think I am. I've been lying and pretending all of this. I'm not a princess. I'm not rich. I shouldn't even be your sons mate. I'm nothing close to the same social status as any of you. I'm a poor girl in a poor family. I do have a sister and a mother. My father is dead. The reason why I even showed up at the party in the first place was because my mother said that she'd sell my little sister and myself if I did not find a rich person at your ball and marry them for their money. I had changed my mind the night of the ball and was going to go home, but it became complicated when your son wouldn't really let me leave once he found out that I was his mate. I am so sorry that I deceived you all. I'd understand if you want to punish me, but please let me at least find another place for my little sister. I can't let my mother sell her when she is only thirteen" Natasha told her the entire truth. Tears slipped down her cheeks as she waited. Waited for the Queen to do something.

The Queen stood up and took Natasha in her arms. "You my girl. Are a sweet, wonderful woman. I'm not going to punish you. You did the right thing by coming out with the truth. I understand why you lied though. It took a lot of courage for you to tell the truth with what was at stake. The only thing is, is that you have to find a way to tell Emen. I'm not really sure how he'll react. One piece of advice is that you have to make sure that you don't give him a chance to break into your explanation. Explain everything as much as possible and at once so it will be easier for him to contemplate everything together instead of things as pieces. He might make assumptions if he doesn't hear the whole thing at once" Linda told her. Natasha nodded and thanked her, hugging her hard.

Natasha wiped her tears away,. "you don't know how thankful I am. Just thank you so much" Natasha told her. They sat down talking for the rest of their time about her real life. The whole truth and nothing but the truth. Natasha and the Queen had a nice talk and laughed and smiled. Natasha knew that she'd miss her very much if Emen decided to reject her and leave her. The door opened and emen came through smiling at seeing the two of them enjoying each others company.

"I see that my two favorite woman are getting along nicely" Emen grinned at them.

"Yes. We were having a great talk. We'll have to have a lot more like them in the future" Linda told them both. Natasha wanted to tell her that it all depended on if she was around in the future, but just agreed.

"Well, time to go" emen smiled at her. Natasha nodded and looked back at the Queen as she was directed out of the room. Linda gave her a reassuring smile and Emen and herself made their way out of the castle and got to the train station. They got their tickets, got on the train, and found seats. She looked down at their hands where their fingers were interlocked and sighed. She knew she'd have to tell him before they made it to her house. She just wanted a few more moments of happiness in case this would be their last time together.

Not The Plan

Natasha bit her lip as she contemplated how to tell him. Emen squeezed her hand reassuringly when he noticed her looking at him. He could probably tell that she was nervous. She needed to calm down before he asked her what was up with how she was acting before she was ready to talk to him. She took in a few breathes. She decided that after she was done calming down then she would tell him. She could prepare herself a good bit of the train ride. Though the train ride only took about two hours to get to her home. "I'm going to go to the washroom. I'll be right back" Natasha told him with a smile.

"Are you sure that you look okay Natasha. You just seem to be" he paused trying to think of the right words. "Not here in a sense. Like you're thinking really hard about things" emen asked her, concerned.

"I am thinking about things. I'll talk to you about them when I get back though. Okay" she asked him with a raised eyebrow. Hoping he'd just drop it there. He just nodded and gave her a smile before she walked off to find the bathroom. She had to go through a couple of train cars to get to one that had a restroom. she walked in after making sure that it was vacant and locked the door. She turned herself to look at the mirror and her reflection. She took a few deep breathes and rested her hands on the counter top. Her dilemma was rushing through her head. If she told him he would either see that she had tried to do good and forgive her or he'd hate her and want nothing to do with her. She had to be a big girl though. She had to just tell him the truth and prolonging it would only making it worse. Especially if she waited until they were married or something. No. she had to stop this and she had to stop it now. She took one more look in the mirror and stepped out of the Restroom and started her way back to her car. There had been one empty car in between hers and the car with the bathroom. She ended being stopped by a man in that car. He seemed vaguely familiar. Then she put together the pieces. He was the older guy who she had danced with at the ball. His name just wouldn't come up in her mind though. She looked down at the hand that her stopped her, which was now circling her wrist.

"It's nice to see you again Natasha" the man told her with a genuine smile.

"I'm sorry, but I've seemed to have forgotten your name" Natasha said apologetically.

"Charles Sanders. The Duke of Warrington" he smiled at her and gave her a little bow. He still didn't let go of her wrist, which she thought was odd.

"Well, it certainly is nice to see you again, but I best be getting back to my set" Natasha said, excusing herself. The hand on her wrist stopped her from exiting the car though. Her eyes darted up to his in an instant. Panic was rising through her body and constricted inside of her. It felt like there was a python coiling around her lungs and constricting slowly, but painfully. "Please get your hands off of me" she said with as strong and authoritative voice as she could. His grip on her didn't loosen a bit. She decided to try another approach. "You are below me. I'll have you beheaded" Natasha told him. Trying to add a threatening tone to her voice. He simply laughed at her. She thought he'd at least be a little afraid of her threat.

"You are very much below me and I think that the both of u know it"
Charles told her with a mischievous gleam in his eyes. She felt her breathing
start to quicken. He couldn't possibly know! "I'm surprised that you don't
remember me dear. I do suppose that I have grown slightly older, but it
hasn't been that much" He was looking at her with a knowing look. Like
she should know what he was talking about? He must be batty out of his
wits.

"I can assure you that I have no clue what you are referring to. You must be
thinking of someone else" Natasha told him as she tried to pry his fingers
off of her wrist.

"No. You are who I am talking about. I'll try to refresh your memory a little
bit. Around the age of ten, you were a girl who liked the outdoors. You
also liked to play in the stable a lot. You helped take care of horses, because
that's what your mother did as a job. Helped clean horses for royalty and
take care of them. This stable was at a Duke's castle. That Duke was me.
From the first day I saw you standing on a post trying to look at the horses,
I just knew that when you were of age you'd have to be mine. Your mother
was desperate for an actual house since your father had died and you three
lived in a shabby little thing with four walls. So, I proposed that when you
were eighteen I would marry you and I'd give her a very nice house to live
in until then and then even after we're married. I told her I'd even give her
even more money once we were married. So, when you turned eighteen
she made up this whole plan for you to go to the ball. You were supposed
to be charmed by me and just agree to marry me. Instead you fell for the
Prince" Charles exclaimed. His grip had tightened quite a bit on the flesh of
her arms. As he was talking she started to remember things. Their shabby
home, playing in the horses stalls, and even him.

"I'll never agree to marrying you" she yelled at him as she hit him with her
other hand. He grabbed her hand and growled. "Don't hit me. I have a very
short temper" he spat out. His body was shaking slightly and there was a

rumbling coming from his chest. "You will marry me" he said slowly after he calmed down a little.

"I will not and you will let me go right now" Natasha yelled at him. He must not know that she has a very short temper also. After struggling with her several moment he just picked her up over his shoulder and started to carry her away from her car on the train. She just started screaming at the top of her lungs. Praying that someone would hear her. Her prayers were answered quite sudden when a door behind them slammed open. She couldn't see who it was because she could only see the Duke's backside. She heard a very loud and ferocious growl coming from her savior.

"Put her down" the voice told him. There was anger seeping into every word. Well, it wasn't exactly anger, because it was quite cold. It was like his voice chilled the air surrounding them all. She knew that voice though. She'd know it anywhere. Angry or not. It was Emen.

"I don't think I will. I basically own her and I will be marrying her" Charles said.

"I don't think that's likely in the least. Now why don't you put her down before I have to tear your arms apart from your body just so you can never touch my mate ever again" Emen's voice, void of emotion now, told him. She knew he was livid, but he just talked like he felt nothing at the moment. He was probably trying to control his anger and not show Charles how much he was bothering him.

The Duke put her down, but made sure that she was behind him and couldn't get past him. "I paid to marry her" Charles stated. He didn't seem like he was going to back down.

"And who may I ask did you pay to marry her" Emen asked her. His voice now held anger in it. He didn't seem like he would be backing down either.

"Her mother. I paid for her house when she was ten when we made this agreement and promised more money when we did actually get married" Charles smirked at him.

"She's a Princess. It's not very likely that she'd need the likes of you to pay for her house" Emen told him. Clearly not believing him.

"But emen. I'm no-" Natasha tried to finally tell him the truth, but Charles interrupted her.

"That is unless she's not a Princess. Which she isn't. I would know. Her mother used to muck out my horses stalls. She's as poor as they get" the Duke sneered. Natasha felt her heart breaking at the look on Emen's face. She could tell that he felt betrayed and there was small hurt there. The emotions flashed across his face quickly before disappearing.

"My mate is coming with me. No matter where she came from or who she is" emen snapped out. Natasha felt relief and her heart soared. He wasn't going to just leave her like she had thought he would! Though this isn't exactly the way she imagined telling him the truth. At least now he knew.

"There isn't a chance of that happening" Charles told him. They were both staring each other down as growls erupted from the two of them right before they both turned into their wolf form. There really wasn't much room in the small train car. She knew right then and there that this would be a fight she could never forget.

A Girl Worth Fighting For

Emen's wolf was huge and pitch black. She had never seen a wolf the size of his. His fur looked soft though. The Duke's wolf looked much smaller in comparison. Duke Charles fur was a dark gray. Much like his human hair. Natasha shuddered at the thought of this man, who could be her grandfather, actually thinking about marrying her. It disgusted her. Emen was very intimidating when in human form and Wolf form. In wolf form he looked vicious though. The two were growling at each other and snapping their teeth. Natasha was sure that Emen would win. He was much bigger and seemed to know what he was doing. The Duke was much older though and probably had more experience with this sort of thing. Natasha prayed that Emen would be okay. The two wolves made the small compartment look even smaller. This would make the fight much harder, because it would be easier for either of them to get more injured than if they were out in the open. Natasha held her breath as Charles attacked emen.

The gray wolf's jaws were opened wide, prepared to tear into the flesh of its opponent and hopefully take his life. Emen was prepared for him though and ducked his body to the side and swiveled his head to the right and clenching his teeth at the base of the Dukes neck. The Duke howled and clawed at Emen's body. Emen's grip loosened on him and the gray wolf moved out of the black wolfs reach. Crimson blood was starting to drench the fur where the flesh had been partially torn open. The Duke growled in fury. He fainted to the left and then went to the right. Emen reacted a little too slow and the gray wolf locked his jaws onto the shoulder of the black wolf. Emen growled and tried to kick at him, but couldn't quite get him, because every time he'd move to dig his claws into him, he'd move just out of reach. Emen flinched when the Duke started to shake his head to tear more of the flesh apart. Emen snapped his head and bit down on his ear and ripped it right off. The Duke yipped and quickly let go of emen. They were quite the sight. Emen's black fur seemed to become impossibly darker on his shoulder and around his mouth. The dukes once pure fur was turning a weird red along the base of his neck, ear (Well, the part left), and around his mouth.

Suddenly Emen pounced onto the Duke. His claws were extended and dragged across the scruffy, gray fur. It left behind bloody marks and a painful howl sounded throughout the small compartment that they were in. Emen aggressively continued his attack. He didn't even pause as he bit into the Duke's shoulder and tearing at the flesh with his razor sharp teeth. She could tell that he was taking out his anger on him. She could hear the gray wolf whimper and try to knock Emen off, but couldn't do it. Emen was panting heavy as he scratched at Charles side and stopped the assault. His breathing hard, muzzle bloody, and satisfaction in his eyes. Natasha slowly walked towards them. She was pretty sure that Emen was done attacking him and she was almost just as sure that the Duke wouldn't want to keep fighting him. Natasha watched as the gray wolf suddenly turned into a very naked man. She averted her eyes to look at the black wolf. She hoped that her eyes showed the love that she felt for him. Though it was just barely there, it was still love.

The duke was suddenly up and was standing behind her. He grabbed a hold of her around the waist and when Emen barked, Charles unsheathed his claws and rested one right above the vein in her neck. She sucked in short breathes when she felt his claw slightly dig into her skin and looked at Emen panicked. Emen's growl was slowly building, rumbling inside of his chest. "Now this is what is going to happen Emen. You are going to back up right now and let us go out the door behind me. You won't try to come after her or I'll kill her. I'll slit her throat right open" The duke's breath was fanning her cheek. Her panic spiked when he started to pull her backwards and Emen just stood there and watched. She didn't really know what she expected him to do though. He opened the door and he pulled her so they stood in between the two train cars. The wind was blowing around them and swaying her hair crazily around them.

"Please don't do this. I don't want to marry you. We'll both be miserable. I just don't want to be with you" Natasha pleaded. She couldn't go with him. She couldn't believe that she was begging him though.

"You might be miserable, but I won't. I've wanted you to be mine for so many years and I will not just let someone else take you from me" he told her. Natasha looked into the compartment that they had just been in. Emen was staring at her, desperate to help her. She still felt the claw against her throat. She wondered if he realized that he was still naked. She shuddered at the thought of his body pressed against hers. She knew that she had to do something. She couldn't just sit there and let him kidnap her. Natasha looked at Emen with sad eyes as she felt a small tear go down her cheek before it was taken away into the wind. She just knew that she couldn't be with this man. No matter what it took. She pulled her hand forward and hit his ear as hard as she could. The next thing she knew she was pushed hard, as he tried to get her away from him and she was pushed right off of the side of the train. She felt the wind pushing against her body, the wind howling as it went by her ears. She heard an ear piercing howl right before she hit the ground hard and everything went black.

~~~A/N~~~

Sorry that it's so short, but I hope that you liked it!
~~~

Showing You Care

"up. You can do it" Natasha heard a familiar voice say to her. All she could see was black. Her eye lids were too heavy for her to actually open them. The voice was comforting and she felt like the person was very close to her. "Baby. Please don't leave me. I need you. I just found you and I need you so much. Open your eyes" the voice told her. The voice was gentle, loving, and firm. She wanted to open her eyes so she could see who the beautiful voice belonged to, but she couldn't get her body to do what her mind was telling her to. She felt her body being picked up. She was on her stomach and something soft was underneath her. She was bent over something. She couldn't be too sure what. She whimpered at the pain that hit her. Pain from all over. Pain from her head, her ribs, and her shoulder. She was pretty sure that she hit just about every part of her body when she had hit the ground.

A small growl came from close by. It was right beneath her. A wolf. Was she being carried by a wolf? Well, her sense of smell told her yes. She breathed in the scent a little more. It was comforting. Natasha suddenly remembered the train ride and all that had gone on. Seeing the Duke again, the two wolves fighting, her flying off of the train. Now she was here and in so much pain. She figured out that it must be Emen and he must be in his wolf form.Had he jumped off of the train? He was apparently carrying her, but to where? They were pretty much in the middle of no where for at least two hours walking both ways. He wouldn't be able to carry her all that way. She ran her fingers through his fur gently, careful not to move too much so that she didn't hurt the rest of her body. Her eye lids were already heavy, but they felt even more heavy. All she wanted to do was sleep. So she whispered "Thank you" right before she slipped back into the darkness.

Natasha could feel herself waking up slowly. She was becoming aware of everything around her. The smell of the room was kind of like a hospital. It was a mix of too clean air, the smell of medicine, and the smell of werewolves. She could hear a beeping sound that would beep every few seconds. She could hear someone quietly snoring not too far away. She felt something in her arm, but wasn't too sure what. She slowly began to open her eyes to look at her surroundings. The room was dim so at least the bright lights wouldn't hurt her eyes. She was in a room that looked kind of like a hospital room. She was laying on a white bed and there were tubes in her arms. She looked at them confused. Why would she need those? She had only probably been here for a few hours at the most and it's not like she was that bad off. Maybe just a broken collar bone or rib, but nothing too serious. She gazed around the room and found the source of the snoring. In a chair that was in the corner was Emen. He was slouching with his legs spread wide apart, his mouth slightly open, and his hair really messy. She found this pretty attractive, even his snoring.

"Emen" Natasha tried to say, but her voice was scratchy and quiet. She tried again, but someone touched her shoulder and made her jump. She looked to the side to see the Queen. Natasha was surprised that she could get here in just a few hours. "What are you doing here" Natasha asked her confused.

"Well, my son called me and told me everything that happened. I tried to convince him to bring you to our home, but he said it would be too dangerous in your condition. He told me that he'd stay here with you and he wouldn't leave this room at all until you were awake. He hasn't left except to go to the bathroom for the past four weeks. Bless his heart. He is such a sweet and caring young man" Linda said. "That's why I'm here. I needed to make sure my son ate and still got his rest. I'm sure he wouldn't have if I hadn't come. Plus, I wanted to make sure that you were alright" Linda told her with a smile and a twinkle in her eyes. Natasha looked at her strangely.

"What do you mean he's been here for four weeks? I just got here" she tried to think of how long she had actually been here "A couple of hours ago" Natasha tried to explain to her, but the Queen shook her head with a sad smile.

"Natasha honey" she said taking ahold of her hand. "You got pushed off of the train and you got beat up pretty badly. You hit your head and you got a concussion. You ended up falling into a coma on the way here. Emen tried to carry you as fast as possible, but he knew that you were in a lot of pain and he didn't want to make it worse" the Queen told her. Natasha looked at her confused. She had just thought that it was just a figment of her own imagination. That she had just made it up in her own mind. "You're a werewolf so you healed within the first week, but you just didn't wake up. You scared Emen pretty badly I can say that. He was running around yelling at different doctors and nurses telling them to take care of you. He made sure that you were their top priority. I can say that the threats he told them weren't exactly polite, but I sort of understand him. He is his fathers son after all" Linda smiled a bit.

Natasha gazed back over at Emen. He was so adorable. The things that she had just told her ran around in her head. He was showing how much he cared. After all that she had put him through. "I think it's best if I wake him up now. I'm sure that he'll be quite angry that I hadn't woken him up just as soon as you had" Linda laughed a little. She walked over and lightly shook Emen's shoulder. He immediately sat up straight and his eyes opened quickly. His eyes found hers and he stood up and went to her side in an instant. He took hold of her hand and started to kiss it.

"I can't believe you're awake. I thought I would lose you" he whispered. His voice was hoarse. Almost as hoarse as her own. His was much more attractive though.

"I can't believe that you stayed here the entire time" Natasha whispered. Her throat was so scratchy and uncomfortable. Emen got her a cup of water and helped hold her up so that she could take a few sips before letting her back down.

"Of course I stayed her. What kind of mate would I be if I just left you when you were hurt" emen asked her.

"Well, I'm not the best mate for lying to you this whole time" Natasha told him ashamed of herself. She turned her head so that she was looking out the window and not at him, but he cupped her chin in his hand and turned her head back to looking at him.

"I haven't known you long, but I can see that you either really regret it or didn't want to in the first place. Just tell me the truth" emen told her. Natasha took a deep breathe. This is what she needed to do. She was sure that he'd understand. He seemed to be very understanding at the moment. She just hoped that this would end better than what she had originally thought.

The Truth Comes Out

Natasha took a deep breath as she stared at Emen. She felt like he truly cared about her. Well, he jumped off of a train, carried her all the way here, and he never left her side for weeks straight. So, he must care right? "I feel like you'll hate me after I tell you this" Natasha told him honestly. Emen squeezed her hand gently.

"I won't hate you. I just want to know the truth. I want to know my real mate" Emen told her with a small smile. He was trying to encourage her and it was working.

Natasha looked down at their hands and began to tell him how this all came to be. "Well, when I was little I had both of my parents. They were both so happy and loving towards each other and towards me. They then had my little sister Bella. Well, my father was killed around when I turned six or so. Ever since then my mother changed. She turned into this horrid woman. It was like she hadn't ever been the kind woman she had been before. She had just changed so much and in a bad way. Maybe it was because of the stress of raising two children on her own. She did have to work in the stalls until that horrible man paid her a whole house just to marry me. She started to say mean things to me and about me all of the time. I began to think that I was worthless. She wasn't as mean to Bella, but she wasn't much better" Natasha paused for a second and then continued. She knew that she couldn't stop or she'd never finish.

"Well, as time passed, my mother became anxious to get rid of us. She kept telling me how much she wanted us to leave and she'd be happy the day that we never came back. A little bit before the ball she had come up with a plan. She told me that I had to go to your ball. She told me that she had set everything up and that I was to pretend to be a Princess from some far away land. I wasn't going to go along with it until she told me that she'd sell Bella and myself to some strange man if I didn't. I would still have refused if it was just me, but Bella was there too. I couldn't have her be sold. She is just thirteen after all. So, I went to the ball and I saw you. I almost knew immediately that you were my mate, but I knew that we couldn't be. Well, I thought we couldn't. I thought you'd find out and have me killed for pretending to be someone that I'm not. So, I tried to stay away from you, but you wouldn't leave me alone. So I ran. I feel like I would never have been able to get away from you if I tried. I ended up going home with you and hoping that you wouldn't find out and here we are" Natasha finished in a whisper. She really wasn't sure how he'd react. She finally looked up to see Emen with an angry expression. He was more livid than she had ever seen anyone in her life. She suddenly wished that she hadn't said anything.

"I'm sorry. I know I lied to you, but I didn't want to. I swear I didn't" she told him. She was trying to calm him down, but he only seemed to get more angry. He took his hands from hers and when she tried to grab ahold of them again and walked swiftly to the wall that was nearest to them and punched a huge hole in it. Cement particles spread throughout the air and she heard two gasps. One from herself and she turned to see the Queen holding her hands in front of her mouth. Natasha noticed the tears streaming down her face. Had she really hurt the two of them that bad? Well, the queen already knew. Maybe she was upset because her son was so upset? "I really am sorry Emen. I truly am" she whispered. She would have tried to hug him or rub a hand down his back to calm him down, but she felt that that would only anger him more.

He suddenly walked over to the bed she was laying on. He seemed a lot more calm. She flinched when he raised his hand up. She had thought he was going to hit her, but instead he cupped her face. He gently rubbed his thumb across her cheek. "I can't believe that anyone would treat another human being the way that woman has treated you. I can't believe that wretched woman would ever think that it was alright to say things like that to my mate let alone think about selling her to some old hag of a man. I'll tell you what. When you start to feel better, we are going to go get your sister. you better hope that when I see her, her throat won't be ripped out. It's going to take all of me not to do it" Emen whispered to her. She could still hear anger, but also pain in his voice. He brushed some hair from her face before kissing her forehead. He took a deep breath. "I need some fresh air. I'll be back in a little bit" Emen promised her before walking out of the room. The queen came over and sat down next to her after she composed herself.

"My son has a bit of an anger problem, but I believe he was right with what he said. Your mother is a terrible human being. No one should ever be treated the way that you were. I can't say that you've had the worst life, but it is a lot worse than what a life should be" she told her. "How about you rest so that you can get your little sister. I'm sure that you'll feel a lot better when you have her" she told her. She squeezed Natasha's hands before getting up and leaving. Natasha closed her eyes and thought back to how angry Emen got. It wasn't at her though. Natasha felt herself slipping back into the darkness and she just hoped that when she woke up, she felt well enough to go see her sister again. She pictured her sisters face right before she fell back asleep.

Anticipation To Desperation

- -

Natasha woke up fairly easy when someone shook her shoulder gently. She opened her eyes to see Emen's staring right back at her. "Good morning beautiful. I know that you really want to go and get your sister so I decided to wake you up and see how you are feeling" emen told her. She could see concern on his face, but he was trying to cover it with a smile.

"I feel one hundred percent better" Natasha told him. She wanted to reassure him that she was just fine and dandy so that she could go and get her sister. She didn't want Bella to be around her mother more than what was necessary.

"I'll go get a nurse to help get all the tubes out of you" Emen told her as he looked at the IV that was inserted into her vein. He quickly left and came back within minutes with a nurse trailing behind him. She wondered how he had managed to get someone to come so fast. Then she remembered what his mother had told her about him ordering the doctors and nurses to make sure that she was their top priority. She smiled apologetically at the nurse. The nurse came over and pulled out everything and put a band aid on her arm so it would not bleed, though it would stop in seconds since she was a werewolf.

"Thank you" Natasha told the woman as she quickly left the room. "What did you tell her" Natasha said, moving her gaze to Emen.

Emen gave her a look of innocence and looked away from her. "I didn't really tell her anything" Emen told her.

"Tell me" Natasha told him.

"I told her that my mate was ready to leave and she better hurry up or she'd regret it" emen told her.

"I can't believe you did that to her! You better go apologize right now. Apologize to every single doctor and nurse that you were apparently quite rude to" Natasha told him.

"It's not that big of a deal" Emen told her with a heavy sigh.

"Yes it is. You can't just act like a jerk to who ever you please. Now you will go apologize or we'll be sitting in this room for quite some time" Natasha told him as she crossed her arms over her chest. She could hear his mom giggling, but she didn't stop glaring at Emen. Emen smiled at her as he walked towards her. He swooped her up in his arms bridal style and walked out into the hall. "Emen! Put me down right now" Natasha yelled as she hit his chest with her fist, which seemed really small compared to his broad frame. She looked up to see that he was still smiling.

"Listen up everyone. My mate told me I had to do this and I realize that she is right. I'm very sorry for the way that I acted. There was no call for it. I hope you all can forgive me" emen said. He then continued to walk down stairs and then outside to a carriage. Well, rich people just seemed to take these things everywhere. Emen set her down on the seat next to him and his mother climbed in with his help.

"I can't believe you just did that" Natasha told him, lightly hitting his chest.

"I only want to please you" emen smiled at her and held her hand. They were riding for about an hour before they finally stopped. When the door opened, she saw the train. "Ready to try this one more time" emen asked her with a raised eyebrow. Natasha nodded and they quickly boarded the train and they were on their way. All Natasha could think about was Bella. She couldn't even sit still from all of her excitement. She just watched out the window as the scenery went by and Emen held her hand. She felt the train stop and saw that they were at her home town. She felt her chest squeeze and it felt like her stomach was clenching. "It's going to be alright" emen whispered in her ear. He could probably tell that she was having quite a bit of anxiety at the moment. She walked with him through the town. They had to walk about a half an hour to get to her home. It wasn't huge like a castle, but the Duke had given them a nicely sized house.

They walked up to the house and Natasha opened the door. She felt odd being in this house once again. She walked in and looked around. It looked pretty much the same. "Bella" Natasha called. She felt like something was off. It must be because she hadn't been here for a while. "Bella" Natasha called a little louder. She walked up to her little sisters room and found her stuff gone. Where had Bella's stuff gone? Maybe she got moved into a different room? She went from room to room. She didn't find any of Bella's things or her own. She ran down the stairs with Emen following. "Bella" she screamed. She got no answer. She ran outside to the back yard. Her mother was gardening. "Where is Bella" Natasha asked her.

"I feel like it's quite rude for you to come to my home and just start yelling questions at me" her mother told her. The woman didn't even look at her as she talked. "If you must know though, your sister isn't here nor will she ever be" her mother said.

"What are you talking about" Natasha asked her. She could feel the anger rising within her.

"Well, I got a visit from the Duke. He had treated us so kindly and you repay him by falling for some prince. I had a debt to pay to him and even though he wanted you, he decided that your sister would do just fine" she said. "So, I hope that you're happy with yourself. Letting your own sister be sold to some man" her mother tssked as she stood up and wiped her hands on her apron. "I have to go make some tea now, so if you'd kindly show yourselves out of my house and off of my property, that would be great" her mother said as she gave them both a dirty look and started to walk off. Natasha felt like the wind was knocked out of her and she couldn't breathe. Her poor little sister. How could this happen. She knew it wasn't her fault though and suddenly only saw red.

Natasha ran at her and pulled her back. It was fairly easy since the woman hadn't expected it. She then pulled back her fist and punched her in the face. She felt her anger coming out and slowly seeping through her actions. She couldn't stop herself from continually punching her. After all these years, she deserved it. "It's not my fault. It never was. It's all your fault! I can't believe you'd do this to her" Natasha screamed at her as she started to choke her. In that moment, she wanted the woman dead. She didn't deserve to live. She was brought back when Emen pulled her off. She tried to fight against him though, but stopped when he wrapped his arms around hers so that her arms were stuck to her sides.

"I will be having you brought to court. You will more than likely be sent to be hung and burn. Enjoy the rest of your miserable days left" emen said as he picked her up and carried her out of the house and started walking back to the train. She hadn't realized that she had been crying until he softly wiped her soaked cheeks. "We'll find her. I promise" emen whispered to her. She sat in his arms and held onto him for dear life as she cried her heart out. She just hoped that they could get to her sister in time.

Doing What's Right

Natasha had finished crying for a while now. They were still walking. Well, he was. He was still carrying her with her arms wrapped around his neck. She was guessing that it was the whole mate thing, but he made her feel so much better. "I'm really sorry about breaking down" Natasha told him as she kept her eyes trained on his shirt so that she didn't have to focus on his face.

"It's very understandable. It's not like you were crying for nothing. You were crying because of all of the hurt that you have been feeling for all of your life. I wouldn't call it breaking down. I'd call it letting everything out. I know that you feel that you have lost your sister for forever, but I promise we will get her back. No matter what it takes" Emen promised her. He kissed her forehead and continued to walk. Natasha wiped her face to get rid of the evidence of her crying as much as possible. She was sure that her eyes were red and puffy and her nose was probably the same.

"I'd rather walk" Natasha told him. She didn't look at him as he put her on her own two feet and let her walk. She felt like he would look at her differently. Like she wouldn't be as strong as she had been. She had let herself go back there and she couldn't stand it. She had grown up to be strong and not let others effect her because of how her mother treated her.

That was the only way to survive in her eyes. Pretend like nothing ever hurt. Then it felt like nothing ever did hurt. She was stopped by a hand on her arm.

"You know that you can trust me right. I'm here for you. You aren't alone anymore Natasha" Emen told her. He was looking into her eyes and as she looked back, she saw no hate or lies. It was the first time in a long time that all she saw in someones eyes, was love. He pulled her into a hug and she let him. She closed her eyes and breathed in his scent. He made her feel comfortable and happy. She pulled away from him and took in a deep breath. "I think the first thing that we should do is find a bathroom or something to get you washed up in" Emen told her. She was confused until she looked down. Her knuckles were covered in blood. "I think you might have broke your mothers nose" emen told her.

"I didn't think that I had hit her that hard" Natasha said with wide eyes as she looked at her hands.

"Now don't you dare feel guilty over doing that. The woman deserved it honestly. You should be glad that I hadn't gotten ahold of her" Emen told her as he took her hands in his. She looked up at him and they kept on walking. They found a small restaurant and went inside. She excused herself and went into the bathroom. There was no one else there. She looked at her reflection in the mirror. She looked like a total mess. Her hair was sticking up every which way. There was grass and twigs with the occasional chunks of mud sticking through out it. She hadn't remembered rolling on the ground, but she must have at some point during the fight. Her face had mud smeared on it and there were tear streaks going through the muck on her face that had dried on the walk. Her eyes were puffy and red along with her nose. She saw a swollen part on her cheek. Had she missed her mother hitting her in the face too? Probably. She hadn't really been paying attention as she tried to pummel her mothers face into the ground. Her clothes were now torn and dirty. Her knuckles had dried blood over them. She sighed. This was going to be a long process.

Natasha moved her head under the sink and ran the water. She rinsed a good bit of all the stuff out. She pumped some soap into her hair and took about twenty pain staking minutes to wash her hair out as clean as she could. She took the flexible bracelet that she had on her wrist and used it as a hair tie to pull her hair up. She then washed her face and her hands the best that she could. She made sure that nobody was in the bathroom before stripping quickly to just her bra and panties. She took some paper towels and wet them and started to wash off her body. She then stuck her clothes in the sink and washed them the best she could. She wrung out the clothes and then stuck them under the hand dryer and stood there waiting for them to dry. When they were just damp she stuck them on again. She looked in the mirror and noticed that she still looked like a mess. She just didn't look like she had stepped out of a lagoon kind of mess. She did notice that a bruise was forming on her cheek. Nothing that wouldn't heal in an hour or two with her being a werewolf. She was pretty sure that she had taken almost two hours doing all of this. She walked out of the bathroom to see emen sitting in a booth by himself. He was staring out the window, but immediately his gaze went to her when she stepped out.

"Well, you look beautiful" emen smiled at her.

"You don't have to lie to me. I saw my reflection in there" Natasha told him.

"You will always look beautiful to me" Emen told her. She didn't see any lie in his eyes. "So, I feel like we should eat before we start on this huge mission of getting your sister" Emen told her.

"Can we just grab something and go. I don't mean to rush, but I took way too long in there. Way longer than I ever should have. I mean I just don't want Bella with that man any longer than she has to be" Natasha told him.

"I totally understand" Emen told her with a smile. He got up and walked right into the kitchen of the restaurant. Did he even realize that there were boundaries to what he could do? Well, he was royalty so it wasn't like anyone would go against him. He returned moments later with a huge bag which she could only assume had food in it. She shook her head at him, but smiled. They walked outside hand and hand and talked on their way to the train. It was actually a very nice moment. They got onto the train and they ate their food as they waited for their stop. She knew exactly where the Duke lived. They finished eating right before their stop. Natasha took a deep breath as they got off of the train. Emen took her hand in his as they walked up to the mansion. It was like a palace in size. He squeezed her hand right before he knocked on the door.

A few minutes went by before a woman answered the door. "Can I help you" she asked them. She was smiling at emen and completely ignoring Natasha.

"Get The Duke" Emen told her in a cold voice. Natasha smiled at the fact that he didn't even seem to really be looking at the woman. Just at the room behind her.

"I will tell him that he has visitors. You can come in and have a seat in the sitting room" the woman flashed him a smile. They both walked in and were escorted into a lovely room. They sat down on a settee together. He held her hand tightly and she smiled at him. They waited about fifteen minutes before the door opened and Charles Sanders walked in.

"Well, it's a pleasure to see the two of you again. How may I help you" he asked as he sat in a chair with a tall back.

"I think that you know what we want" Emen told him. He was cutting straight to the point.

"I think we all know that what you want won't come without a price" Charles told them.

"What would you like" Natasha asked him. "We'll give you anything. I just want my sister to be safe with me once again. You don't need her. You can have anyone else. She's just a child" Natasha snapped at him.

"You know. You're right. I don't really want her. I do want something else though. You did say that you'd give anything for your dear little sister. Right" he asked her with a raised eyebrow.

"Anything" Natasha told him.

"Your hand in marriage" The Duke said with a twinkle in his eye.

~~~A/N~~~

So, I wanted to apologize for not posting for a bit. I've been very sick and still am. I also had writers block so I'm hoping that this was an okay chapter. :)
~~~

The Bargain

"Why would I do that" Natasha asked him. "We could just have you put in jail or worse" Natasha told him coldly. Nobody messed with her sister or herself.

"Well, that wouldn't really help your sister now would it? All I have to do is call one person and they'll snap her little neck" Charles smiled at the two of them.

"And if I were to snap yours before you could even reach for your phone" Natasha asked him.

"Well, you don't know where she is and it's a very hard place to find. So, she'd probably starve and die before you got to her" The Duke smirked at her.

"I could smell her out" she told him.

"See. Now there is another problem for the two of you. I actually already thought about that. I gave her different clothes to change into and the room that she is in is a seal and lock kind of room. So, her scent won't be leaking out of that room anytime soon. We have actually spent quite the amount of money to make the entire palace smell different since she's moved in" The Duke told her.

"So, how is this going to go then? There is no way that I'll agree to marrying you if you still have my sister and I'm pretty sure that you won't just let my sister go and trust that I'll actually marry you" she said. She was feeling pretty much defeated at this point. she knew she'd have to marry him to save her sister, but she just hoped that he'd be true to his word and let her sister go at some point.

"Actually. I'll let your sister go immediately with the Prince boy here as long as you agree to one condition" Charles said.

She took a deep breath. "What is your condition" Natasha asked him.

"You have to wear an ankle monitor. I will not have you just running off on me before the wedding now can I" he asked her with a condescending smile.

"No I guess we can't have that. If you let my sister go right now, then I agree" Natasha told him.

"What? You can't do this Natasha! We can find another way" emen practically yelled. She could tell that he was panicking.

"I'll go get her and the monitor" The Duke said. "I'll be expecting you to still be here when I get back" he said before walking out of the room.

Emen grabbed her by the shoulders. "What are you thinking" Emen said as he looked into her eyes. She could see the hurt and desperation in his eyes.

"You want to know what I'm thinking? I'm thinking about saving my little sister okay! That is what I'm thinking about right now. I'm not stupid. I have sort of a plan to go with it. I will go along with this and at the wedding, which I'm sure he will announce to every kingdom around so you'll know when it is, you can come and save me with a whole army. Please don't think that I want to do this, because I most definitely don't, but it's what I have to do. Unless you can come up with a better plan, then this is what we're doing and you better save me, because I don't know what I'm going to do if I'm stuck for life with that man instead of you. You mean the world to me and it's tearing me apart to do this and you better keep my Bella safe" Natasha told him and grabbed his face in her hands and pulled his face to hers so that she could kiss him with as much love as she could show in one kiss. She pulled back. "I love you" she whispered. She knew it was her first time ever telling him this, but she just hoped that it wasn't her last.

"I love you too and I promise you that I will keep her safe" he whispered back and kissed her one last time before the Duke re-entered the room and he brought along her sister and in his hand was the monitor. She was going to dread wearing that stupid thing. There was no way that she'd be able to escape now.

"So, here is the precious little Bella. Emen and her can leave now so that my fiancée' and I can plan our wedding together" Charles said as he shooed Bella over to Emen and pulled Natasha up by her hand to stand by him. She felt disgusted that he was touching her at all. Emen gave her a longing look and the Duke a heated one as he grabbed Bella's hand and went to go walk away. Bella tore her hand away from Emen and ran over to Natasha.

"I missed you so much Tasha. When am I going to see you again" she asked looking up at her. Natasha hugged her back and felt tears well in her eyes as she looked down at her.

"Hopefully really soon you can come visit or something" Natasha told her. Emen came over and pulled Bella to him and she squirmed as she tried to get away from him.

"I want Tasha" she screamed as she tried to get away.

"Bella. Go with her honey. That's Emen. He's very nice and will take care of you while I'm not there okay" Natasha told her. There were tears running down Bella's face.

"But I want you. Only you" Bella cried out.

Natasha's heart was wrenching in her chest. She just wanted to run away with Bella and Emen so bad at that moment. "Bella. Listen honey. I wish I could be with you right now, but I have to do some stuff first. I'll see you really soon okay? I need you to be a big girl. you're thirteen now and I know you're afraid right now, but I need you to be strong and go with Emen for me" Natasha told her. She could tell that Bella didn't want to go, but she slowly nodded.

"I love you Tasha" Bella told her.

"I love you too Bella Bear" Natasha told her. Emen wrapped his arms around her little sister and she cried into his shoulder as he gave Natasha one last look before leaving. Natasha felt like there was a boulder sitting in her stomach. She couldn't believe she had to watch her sister get taken away. At least this time it was a man she trusted with her life taking her. She sat down heavily on the couch that was closest.

"So, now that they're gone. Time to put your anklet on and then we can get started with our life together" The Duke smiled at her. She felt numb. It was like she wasn't even in her own body. She never felt him putting the ankle monitor on or him kissing her cheek as he went to go get a planner or something. All she could think of was her little sister and Emen.

"Please Emen. You better keep Bella safe and come and save me as fast as you can" Natasha whispered to the empty room around her. She just hoped that this wouldn't be as much torture as she thought it would be.

~~~A/N~~~
~~~

So, I am feeling much better. Thank you all who sent me messages and comments hoping that I'd feel better. I really hope you guys like this chapter. I'm really excited about this story and I can't wait to get to the wedding because there will be a lot of action. It's something to look forward to ;) Thank you all for reading!

Trapped

Natasha is sitting in a huge dining room. If that's what you could call it anyways. It seemed more like a hallway with a huge table with a million chairs. She couldn't actually imagine having a party where she'd need this big of a room to eat in. She was sure that two hundred people could fit into this one room quite easily. She was stuck right next to Duke Charles, the ankle monitor weighing heavily on her ankle. She could understand why he had put it on her, but she just was frustrated that she was in this situation to begin with. If he had just left her alone and found someone his own age, this wouldn't be happening right now. She would be with Emen and Bella right at that moment. She could see them having dinner and laughing about some past memories together. She was brought back to some coughing. She looked over to her left where the duke sat at the head of the table. "I find it kind of rude for you to be day dreaming when you are having dinner with me" Charles told her.

"I'm sorry that I don't exactly find it a pleasure to be eating with someone who threatened me and the ones I loved and are forcing me to marry you" Natasha told him, disgusted. She didn't understand how anyone could do this to anyone else. It was despicable.

"I'm not forcing you to do anything. I gave you the choice and you chose to do this" Charles told her.

"No. You never gave me a choice. You knew that leaving my sister here was never a choice for me. You knew that the only choice I would ever pick was being stuck with an arrogant jerk like you. I don't see how you can even live with yourself. You are truly pathetic for ever thinking that any of this was ever okay. You should have just left me alone, because I'm going to make your life a living hell" she told him coldly. She was looking at him straight in the eye and never looked away. He did though and coughed a little bit. Food was brought in to them. It was way more than they would ever be able to possibly eat just the two of them. He was probably just trying to impress her. She wasn't really sure as to what the best way to make his life a living hell would be. She could tell that he was watching her as she looked at all the food. She decided that the best way for right now, was to disgust him. Make him so disgusted with her that he would never even think about wanting to marry her.

Natasha reached forward and grabbed some barbecue chicken with her hands and just started eating. She could feel that she had the sauce all over her lips, her cheeks, and she was pretty sure that when she had went to move her hair to the side she had even gotten some on her forehead. She filled her cup up with some sort of bubbly beverage. It was sprite. She chugged it in a few gulps and belched as loud as she could make herself. She wiped her mouth slightly on the back of her hand. She suddenly pictured him kissing her and quickly reached for the closest food that would make her breath smell disgusting and repulsive. Her hands connected with pork chops that are covered in sauerkraut and onions. She ate mostly the sauerkraut, even though it made her feel sick. She took another swig of the soda before placing down her cup and sighing. She rearranged herself so that she was sitting sideways in the chair with her legs over the side and onto the chair next to her own chair. "Well, that was just fantastic" Natasha told him. She glanced over at him to see his reaction. It was a look of pure shock. He probably expected her to threaten to starve herself or maybe it was just the fact that no one had ever acted that unladylike near him. Well, that wouldn't be the last time that this sort of thing would happen if he kept her here.

"So, I take it that you liked the food" Charles asked her.

"Yes. It was very good even if the company was not. So, I'm pretty tired from this whole day. Where is my room" Natasha asked him.

"Well, I'll show you where our room is" he told her. She looked at him like he was crazy. If the pervert actually thought that she would ever share a room with him, then he was even more crazy and senile than she had originally thought.

"Our room" Natasha asked him just to clarify as she also stood up.

"Yes, we'll be sharing a room" he said looking at her.

"Yeah? I really don't think so. I'm a lady" she said. She found a lot of humor in this one statement just because of how she had acted moments before. "I will not share a room with a man unless he is my husband" she told him.

"Well, let me go get a preacher and we'll get that settled then" he told her. She could tell he was getting frustrated, but she honestly didn't care.

"No! We have to have a huge wedding. I want everyone to be there. I've always dreamed of having a big wedding when I get married. Lots of people" Natasha told him. She wanted to make sure as many people as possible could be there so it would be easier for emen to get in some how.

"Fine. We'll be getting married really soon. Within the month" Charles said, angry. He walked with her to a door. He opened it and showed her inside. It was a huge room. "This is a guest room. You can spend the night in here until we are wed. When we get married though, you will be with me in our room" he told her sternly.

"Of course" she said rolling her eyes and huffing. She couldn't believe she was stuck in here. At least she wasn't stuck in "their" room. He looked at her for once second in disgust before he put on a cool mask.

"Go clean up. I'll be waiting for when you're done" he told her. Natasha looked at him. She didn't really feel like listening, but was worried that he'd force her to sleep in his room if she didn't listen. She walked into the bathroom that was attached to her room. She washed her face and sighed as she looked in the mirror. She wished that she could be trapped in the bathroom alone instead of being around him. He was a horrid man. She shook her head as she dried her face and walked back into her room. There was a night gown on the bed.

"You can leave now. I'm ready to sleep" Natasha told him. Natasha looked over at him when he didn't move. He walked closer to her. Close enough to where there was barely any space in between the two of them. She backed up and he followed her until her back hit the wall. "What are you doing" Natasha asked him.

"I'm going to kiss my fiancée goodnight" he replied as he looked down at her lips. He put a hand under her chin and lifted her face up. She struggled to get her face out of his grip, but it was too strong.

"Let me go. I don't want to kiss you" Natasha snapped at him. She pushed at his chest with as much strength as she could, but with him being a male werewolf, he was much stronger. He pushed himself closer to her and bent his head down and pressed his lips to hers. She tried to shake her head so that their lips would no longer have contact, but she couldn't move her head an inch. He licked her bottom lip, asking for entrance. She denied him and he pulled her hair with a soft jerk until she gasped and slipped his tongue inside of her mouth. She bit his tongue as hard as she could. She could taste the blood seeping into her mouth. He suddenly jerked back with a yelp. Blood dripped down his chin. It reminded her of the fact that he was missing his ear.

"You little wench" he snapped and slapped her hard with the back of his hand. She was knocked onto the floor and her vision was blurry. She heard the door slam and she felt her vision turning black. She couldn't believe that she had let anyone kiss her besides her mate. She couldn't believe how weak she was. "Emen. Please forgive me" she whispered as a tear slipped from the corner of her eye and she let the darkness over come her.

~~~A/N~~~

I know this chapter isn't all that exciting, but I need some fill in chapters and you guys can see how they are acting towards each other. I hope you guys are all still interested in it. I love all of you for taking the time to read this book! :)
~~~

The Plan

Emen paced back and forth in front of his parents and Natasha's little sister. He was so angry with himself because he couldn't stop this from happening. "Hey honey. I think that you should go for now. I'll send you to the kitchen with Bridgette and you and her can get something to eat okay" Linda, his mom told Bella. She looked over at Emen and he nodded her head before she agreed. The two left for a moment before his mother came back in alone and shut the door quietly and calmly behind herself. "You can tell us about what happened now. I didn't want you to scare the poor girl off. Her sister left her in your hands so you're the only one she probably truly trusts at all here" she told him. Emen nodded his head and turned to the two of them.

"So, here we are trying to get Bella from her mother. Her mother already sold her to Charles. Natasha beat her mother to all living hell. I'm sure she broke her nose. We went to stop at a diner and she washed up. We then went to go to the Dukes home. He said that we had to trade Natasha for Bella. I didn't want to, but Natasha wouldn't let Bella stay there for another minute. If he touches her I swear that he will live a very painful life. Full of broken bones and non-life threatening wounds" Emen practically yelled as he started to pace again. His mother stopped him with a hand on his arm.

"Do you know what you do" she asked him. "You go and save her. You aren't alone here. You have us and a whole army of people. We love that girl who seems to have stolen your heart even though we have only known her a short period of time. We will help you fight for her. What ever you need, we'll get. If you don't have a plan, then we'll help you come up with one" she said as she put both her hands on his shoulders.

"Well, Natasha came up with a good part of a plan. She said that during their wedding I could come save her. They would invite a lot of people, so we can know the day and time. I just have to save her before they say I do" Emen said.

"And you will. We can have the whole army attack at once" Linda told him.

"No" Emen said. "He'd be expecting that and it would be quite obvious that we're all there" Emen said. He was sure that the Duke had some sort of army of his own. He had no doubt that his army could over throw the Duke's, but he didn't want any chance of him hurting his mate.

"What if you were to sneak in with a couple of highly trained men. You can pretend to be guests and make sure that Natasha is safe before all the rest show themselves. Then we can have more men come in after getting a call or something" his father suggested. Emen nodded his head as he thought about it. It was a pretty logical plan, but they'd need to get into more details with it. He would not mess up this plan. He had to keep Natasha safe at all costs. His plan would work, no matter the cost.

~~~Natasha's POV~~~

Natasha sighed as she put her elbow on the table and her chin rested in her hand. They had been planning the wedding for hours upon hours with almost no breaks. She didn't want to get married in the first place, let alone
~~~

making plans for it. There were so many florists and designers that she couldn't keep any of them straight. One person would ask about what kind of flowers she wanted. She just said roses. Then they would ask what color and she'd say white. Then another would as for the color of the table settings for the reception and she said blue. The list went on and on as they picked out every single detail for the wedding. It was driving her absolutely insane. By the time that Emen came and saved her, she'd have to be put into an insane asylum. "How many guests would you like to come" one person asked. He was a very well dressed man with glasses that made him look more distinguished than geeky.

"I want many, many guests. As many as possible. If I am going to get married then I want everyone to know and be there. Send invitations to every town around. Everyone is invited" Natasha stated. This is the one topic that she actually cared about. There had to be many people there or else her plan just wouldn't work out. She was sure that Emen would figure out something either way. The man looked over at the Duke to confirm that this was alright. It was a little odd that she wasn't setting a perimeter of the number of guests they would be having.

"If it makes her happy, then I'm happy" Charles said smiling. He seemed to be happy that she seemed to perk up a little. She hadn't smiled once that day except for right then. She just couldn't help smiling when she thought about Emen coming to rescue her. Though she imagined him coming to save her on a white steed and she knew it would never happen, but it was a very nice thought.

"Great. I can think of a few other things that would make me very happy and pleased" Natasha smiled at him. She was pretty sure that she could actually enjoy this a bit and make it a lot easier for her to escape. "I want several white horses placed around the room. Well, just one of them ac-tually. I think white horses are elegant and nice. I also don't want to wear heels. They are very uncomfortable and I'd rather be comfortable for the wedding. Plus, you aren't that much taller than me. I'd hate it if I were suddenly taller than you. Especially on our wedding day. How embarrassing" Natasha told him. She was surprised when he agreed. Especially when she had just insulted him. This was just the beginning of her plans and she was sure that they would work.

The Wedding (Part I)

~ ~~A/N~~~

So, I hope that you all enjoy the story so far. This chapter should be pretty interesting to read. I hope you all love it along with the second part! There will probably be a third part as well. :)

It's the day of the wedding and as she stared at her reflection in the mirror, she could see a calm looking woman staring back. She knew that on the inside she was freaking out though. Practically breaking down. Her tan skin contrasted with her long white dress. Her brown hair was pulled up in a tight bun. She knew that she had to go on with this, because it was the only way to make this all work out. She just had to make sure that the ceremony went as slow as possible so that Emen would have enough time to come and save her. She took a deep breath and allowed some girl to put some blush on her cheeks and some lipstick on her lips. She thought that she looked funny, but they assured her that she looked beautiful. It didn't really matter though, because this wasn't going to be her real wedding. During her real wedding, she would actually look beautiful.

Natasha slipped her feet into some white flats. They were cute, but that wasn't why she wanted to wear them. She wanted shoes that she could run in. She felt someone putting the veil on her head and it flowed over her face. She had never saw the point in veils when they'd just be lifted up minutes later. She hoped that Emen would be on his way. She would kill him if she had to kiss that wretched old man again. He was completely vile and she couldn't stand him. She couldn't even believe that he dared to hit her. Speaking of which, she had a nice bruise to show for it. He had made sure to order the girl doing her make-up to make sure that it was covered for the wedding though. She didn't know who he was kidding. No amount of make-up would cover up the dark purple bruise he had given her. She slowly and lightly ran her finger across it. She couldn't change the past, but she could change the future.

"Time for you to get going" a man said behind her. She looked at his reflection in the mirror. She didn't know who he was and was pretty sure that she had never seen him before. "I know you're nervous, but everything will be okay. You may need to buy some time, so we can walk slowly up the aisle" he told her. There was something about the way that he said it. Like he knew her plans.

"Who are you" Natasha asked him, confused and curious.

"I am Tyler and I'll be walking you down the aisle" he smiled at her. She turned to actually look at him. "You look lovely" he told her. She didn't really believe him, but thanked him anyways.

"So, why would you care about me wanting to take my time" Natasha asked him.

"I can see that you're having a hard time with all of this and I'm here to make sure that you are safe" Tyler told her. She sighed as her gaze turned hard. Of course. The Duke had sent him to make sure that she wouldn't run.

"Let's just get this over with" she told him. She walked out past him and to the double doors where the wedding ceremony was being. She felt her hand being put into the crook of Tyler's arm.

"I'm here to help you" he told her quietly.

"Help me by making sure that I get to the end of the aisle" she told him. "I don't call that much help." She didn't even look at him, but she heard him sigh heavily.

"Just stay strong" he whispered to her. She ignored him and took one more deep breath right before she heard an organ playing "Here comes the bride." She never had liked this tune. It was rather annoying. She felt Tyler squeeze her hand before they started making their way down the aisle. They both went at a slow pace. If she didn't know better, she would think that he was going even slower than what she was. It was like he was really trying to get them to go slower. Maybe he was trying to prolong the agony of this whole thing for her. Well, it helped her in a way. It gave Emen more time to come and save her. She searched the crowd around them for emen. She didn't spot him and her heart sank slightly. She knew that he had to come. He just had to.

Though the walk up the aisle was a lot longer than it should have been, it wasn't close to long enough. Tyler put her hand in the Dukes. She grimaced as she felt his wrinkly, clammy skin on hers. She had never been more disgusted in her life until right then. Charles pulled her closer as Tyler stood as the best man. "You look beautiful. I can't wait until I see how beautiful you are tonight" he whispered in her ear. She shuddered and changed her mind. Now this was the most she had ever felt this much disgust in her life. She scanned the crowd with her eyes once more before turning towards the priest. She felt light headed, her stomach was churning, and she felt like her lungs were being crushed in an iron fist. There was no way that she could go through with this to the very end.

"We are gathered here today to" the priest started to drone on and on. All she could think of was her little sister and emen. Her little sister would be safe with Emen, even if he didn't come in time to save her from this terrible event. She knew that she could trust Emen. She wouldn't have let her go with him if she didn't think that he'd protect her and keep her safe and happy. She was jolted back to reality when her hand was squeezed hard.

"I'm sorry. Can you repeat that" Natasha asked him. The priest gave her an odd look.

"Just pay attention" Charles hissed at her. Apparently he hadn't even said anything directed towards her. The Duke had just noticed that she had been zoning out.

"Now. Does anybody object" the priest asked. Everyone looked around, including herself. She felt her heart drop into her stomach as she didn't notice Emen stepping forward or Emen at all. She turned her gaze just in time to see Tyler with a gun pointed at the Dukes head. "I object" his voice rang out across the church. Her jaw dropped as she turned her gaze to the church and saw other men around the room with guns pointed at men who seemed to be guards of the Dukes. "I object as well" Emen spoke out as he slowly started to walk up the aisle. Her heart soared as she looked at him. Their eyes connected right before she felt a sharp pain in her side. She looked down to see a dagger sticking out of her body, right below her ribs and a crimson red color flowed across her pure white dress.

The Wedding (Part II)

~ ~~Emen's POV~~~

E men stood outside of the Duke's palace. He knew that this was where the wedding was going to take place. He was determined to get Natasha back at all costs. He loved her more than he could ever say. Words just couldn't be used to describe the love that he felt for Natasha. He was wearing a very dashing suit and a hat that looked nice and would keep his identity hidden. He just needed to keep hidden until the perfect time to strike arose. He had men all around. They knew the plan of attack. They were all mostly inside of the building right now, positioned right near the Duke's guards. He had a right hand man on the inside. His name is Tyler. Tyler was supposed to walk Natasha up the aisle and then take a hold of the Duke for him. Tyler had pretended to be friends with the Duke so that this plan could be played out correctly.

Emen decided that it was an okay time to go inside, so he did. He walked into the room and blended in with the people around him. Most seemed like snobs, but it seemed like there were more people than just royals. So, Natasha must have had some sort of discussion about wanting more people or something. There were definitely some people who were of lower status then others. A man stops him and Emen just barely glances up to see one of the guards. "Excuse me sir. Can you tell me who you are and where you're from" the guard asked him. Emen felt his heart beating erratically in his chest. It felt like it was going to leave an imprint on his rib cage. His stomach was wrenching and he was afraid that he'd lose his last meal all over the front of the guard. If this guard somehow figured out who he was, then he could ruin all of the planning that he had done to rescue the love of his life.

- -

"My name is Jack Sanders. I live in the town of Holbrook. It's a pleasure to meet you on this fine day" he said and took a quick little bow. The guard looked at him a little strange.

"Why are you here" the guard asked him.

"Well, I'm not here to have a birthday party am I? I'm here for a wedding. The wedding of a beautiful couple. They invited so many people from the towns around here and I happen to be one of them" Emen tried to act like he was upset that the man had asked him who he was and why he was there. He was really freaking out on the inside though.

"I 'm sorry sir. Enjoy the wedding" the guard told him and the guard walked away with one of his men following him. Emen sighed and felt himself calm down a little bit. That was so close. Emen stayed in the back of the room until he heard gasps and saw some of the Duke's guards with guns on them from his men. He wished that he could see all of his men with their guns on all of the guard. The look on their faces would have been priceless. He stepped out into the aisle to see The Duke being held at gun point by Tyler with a look of surprise that turned to pure hatred at the sight of him. Emen turned his eyes to Natasha. She was so beautiful. He started to make his way up the aisle and towards his woman. Emen took off his hat as he walked and he was getting more and more excited to see her. He had to watch as the Duke pulled out a dagger and stabbed Natasha in the side. Things blurred as he ran to the stage yelling. He wasn't sure exactly what he was yelling, but he knew that it had an effect on people, because people were running out of his way as he charged onto the little stage that the duke, Natasha, and Tyler were on. He went straight to Natasha who had blood soaking through her white dress. She was on the floor breathing heavily. She yelled at Tyler to take the Duke to his Dungeon and make sure that he was watched. He picked up Natasha and ran to his horse. He had someone else hold onto her so that he could get on his horse and then held Natasha in his arms again.

<hr>

Emen rode as quickly as possible and tried not to move her around too much. He noticed that the dress was turning more and more red by the second. He pushed on. He made it to his castle a bit later. He knew that the horse he had ridden so hard was exhausted. He jumped off of the horse with Natasha whose eyes were closed. "Come on Baby. Hold on for me. I need you. I'm trying so hard. If you live then I'll marry you right away. I'll protect you and never let anyone hurt you ever again. Please baby. Live for me" he told her as tears fell. His heart was wrenching at the sight of her. Covered in blood and body limp. He gave the reigns of the horse to a servant and ran inside to the doctor that lived there. He was told to put her on the exam table and he was shooed out of the room. He paced back and forth in front of the room. He was freaking out so much right now. He wouldn't be able to live if she died. The door opened about two hours later and the doctor came out and shut the door. "Is she going to be okay" Emen asked him.

"I don't really know. She lost a lot of blood and I managed to stop the bleeding, but her heart is very weak right now. During the next three days we should be able to tell if she will get better" the doctor told him.

<hr>

"But she's a werewolf. She has to live. All werewolves heal easily" Emen told him. He couldn't stand the thought of losing her.

"""Even werewolves have their limit your majesty" the doctor said. "She'll need to rest. Come back in the morning and you can see how she's doing." Emen nodded his head even though he wanted nothing more than to run into the room and hold his Natasha in his arms. He walked away and down to the dungeons. He found the cell that the Duke was in. He growled when he saw him. He felt anger boiling under his skin at the mere sight of this pathetic excuse of a man. He snatched the keys from the guard and he unlocked the cell door and opened it with force. The only sound heard was his heavy breathing and the metallic clang of the door slamming against the wall. He strode forward in quick strides and his hand made contact with his throat. He pulled him up by his neck and squeezed until he could barely breathe.

"Now you listen to me and you listen well. She is the love of my life. The one that I care about most. I'm telling you right now that you will end up dead. Now, if Natasha lives then it will be a short but painful death. If she dies though, you'll wish that you can turn back time, because it will be the most painful and slowly drawn out death anyone could ever experience" Emen growled out the words and dropped him to the ground. He was wheezing and holding his throat as air swiftly flowed once again. "She better live" he told him as he turned around and walked out of the cell. He told the guard to lock him back up and threw him the keys. He made his way upstairs to his room and stared out his window. There was no way that he could get any sort of sleep for the next three days or until he knew that his girl would survive this. He needed her to survive.

Please Don't Go

~ ~~A/N~~~

There will be violence and torture in this chapter. I will put ******
before the part starts so you'll know where to skip if you'd rather not read
about it. I'm sorry that it has taken me so long to update, but I've been very
busy lately. I hope you all enjoy.

~~~Emen's POV~~~

Emen stayed by her side for three days. He paced, held her hand, laid down
next to her and held her, and even just sat in a chair and watched her. He
wouldn't eat or drink anything until the doctor told him that Natasha
wouldn't be happy if she woke up and he was almost starved to death.
So, here he was late at night, eating ham and drinking water as he looked
out the window. He finished eating and put down his plate and cup and
walked over to Natasha. He ran his fingertips across her cheek lightly. He
watched as her chest slowly moved up and down at the steady rhythm of
her breathing. Her lips were slightly parted and air entered and left there.
He took hold of her hand and studied it. It was so small, delicate, and soft.
She was just so fragile.
~~~

It has been three days and the doctor said that they should know if she will live or not by if she wakes up this day or not. He felt his eyes well up with tears at the thought of Natasha not waking up. He griped her hand a little tighter. "Baby. Please wake up. I need you. I need you to live. I need you to be here by my side. I need you to be my wife and have my children. I just need you. You mean more to me than I ever thought any person would. I know that I haven't told you how much I love you and that will change. I will tell you every single day. I won't let a day go by without telling you how much you mean to me. I just need you to come back to me honey. Please. Baby please don't go" Emen told her and kissed her face as tears fell down his. His heart was aching so much from the thoughts that he was having. His thoughts of her dying and being buried.

He knew right then and there that if she did die what he would do. He'd go and kill the man in the cell as slowly and painfully as possible before killing himself. Natasha was his life ever since he met her. Being her mate was the best thing that ever happened in his life. She was just his everything. "I probably need a shower, but I don't think your tears are going to clean me" Natasha's voice croaked out. He jumped back and looked at her surprised at seeing her eyes open and watching him.

"You're awake. You're alive" Emen said confused, excited, and happy all mixed together.

"Well, yeah I am silly. How long have I been out for" Natasha asked him as she swiped at her eyes to clear the sleep.

"For three days. The duke stabbed you and you lost a lot of blood" Emen told her as he wiped his tears off of her face and his own. "The doctor said that even though you're a werewolf, you could have died. your body has just taken so much in such a short period of time and I was so worried that I'd lose you. You mean the world to me baby. You mean more than words can ever explain" Emen told her and then kissed her on her lips. When he pulled away, he saw the surprise on her face. "You will be told by me each and every day how much I care about you. I swear" emen told her.

"I love you too" she told him with a soft smile as the doctor came in.

"I see that someone is awake and smiling" the doctor said with a smile of his own. "Prince. I'm going to ask you to leave so that I can check on everything" the doctor said. Emen growled at him, but Natasha put her hand on his arm.

"It's fine. It should only take about an hour or so for him to check me over and ask all of the questions. You probably need to go to the bathroom and eat and things. You can get me water before you come back though if you wouldn't mind" Natasha told him.

"Of course sweetheart" Emen told her and kissed her forehead before sighing and walking out of the room. He suddenly remembered what he could do with his time. He had to take care of some trash in the dungeons. He walked all the way down the stairs. His mood went down quite a bit., He wasn't as livid as he had been earlier, but he was still very angry. His mate could have died and it would have been the twit in the cells fault. Emen walked all the way down stairs and to the cell where the duke was at. He turned on the lights and peered through the cell doors. The duke was just laying there on the grimy floor. He was pretty thin now. Emen had made sure that he was fed and watered only enough for him to survive. Emen would not allow him to eat all that he wanted or the good food. He got scraps that weren't even fit for dogs to have.

He glanced at the dukes wrists which were locked in shackles made out of silver. He could see the skin around the shackles blistered and bloody. He could only imagine what the skin looked like beneath the shackles. He could see that for a werewolf who was usually very tan, the Charles looked very pale. His skin was slightly sunk in and you could see parts of his ribcage sticking out through the holes in his clothing. Well, the tattered pieces left of the clothing. There was a stench in the air. He was sure that it was a mix between the mans urine and the smell of the flesh on his wrists. "Well, today is the day. I'm ending your life" Emen told him. He decided not to tell him whether Natasha had lived or not to let him not know how long his death would take to come.

*******Violence/Torture********

Emen grabbed a pair of gloves off of a table and opened the cell door. "You know. I would have thought that you would have just left her alone after you pushed her off of the train. You clearly don't care about her all that much if you're willing to hurt her then and also stabbing her" Emen said. He studied the man laying there. He could see fear fill his eyes as Emen walked closer to him. He squatted down in front of him. "Look. You should have took me coming after her as a warning. You should have just let her go, but you didn't. The reason why this is going to happen to you is because of you and only you. If you would have left her alone and if you would have not hurt her, then we wouldn't be here right now. You'd be living tomorrow" Emen told him.

"Well, she kissed me at my palace. She's pretty good at her. She has a pretty nice body too" the duke chuckled. His laughing turned into grunting and coughing as he tried to get air when Emen punched him in the gut.

"You and I both know that she wouldn't kiss you by choice" Emen said as he stood up and unlocked the mans shackles. Emen knew that he wasn't strong enough to run away or fight him. He walked outside of the cell and grabbed an object that looked like a really long nail, but it is made out of silver. The nail goes from his wrist to his elbow in length. It was very sharp on one end. He walked back into the room the Charles. He looked at the skin where the shackles had been and almost grimaces. There was a lot of blood, but it was like you could see parts of his tendons and muscles. He slowly traced lines across his skin and watched as blisters immediately appeared and the Duke hissed in pain. "I don't take someone hurting my girl lightly" emen told him.

"Just get it over with" the duke told him. Emen looked at him and pierced his skin right below the rib cage so that it was pointing up towards his heart and pushed it up enough so that it would stay without him holding onto it. Blood squirted and started pouring out. The duke howled in pain and tried to grab it out but Emen stopped him by smashing his hand until he heard a sickening pop. The Duke screamed again.

"Well, I thought I should let you know that Natasha did in fact live from you trying to kill her" Emen told him.

"I thought you said that my death would be short if she lived" the duke choked out.

"Trust me. This is fast compared to how long I would have stretched it out if she had died" Emen told him. He looked into his eyes. He then drew back his foot and kicked the silver spike as hard as he could and it pierced into the mans heart. He had the guards clean up the mess and walked back up stairs. No one would ever hurt his mate ever again.

The End For Now

(One Month Later)

~~~Natasha's POV~~~

Natasha looked at herself in the mirror and moved side to side. "I just don't know if I look all that great. I mean this is our first time on an actual date or anything" Natasha looked skeptically at her outfit. It was a blue summer dress and a pair of flats.

"You look amazing" Bella told her for about the hundredth time in the past hour. "You need to stop worrying so much. I mean he seemed to be pretty attracted to you with your hair all wild and bruises all over so I'm sure he'll fall all over himself when he sees you like this" she smiled at her sister.

"I guess you're right. I mean I have to get going. I'm already five minutes late" Natasha said looking at the clock and fixing her hair quickly, even though it was perfect and smiled at her sister. "Than you for all of the help" she told her with a smile.

"No problem" Bella smiled back as Natasha opened the door. "By the way" Bella stopped her before she walked out. "Don't forget to breathe" Bella
~~~

told her. Natasha noticed that she had been holding her breathe and smiled as she inhaled quickly.

"Thank you" Natasha yelled as she ran out of the room, down the hall, down the stairs, and outside to the gardens. She made it to an area that was surrounded by rose bushes. It had a table with a white cloth on it, candles, and silver dishes which probably held their food. There were many stars lighting up the sky. It was so romantic and beautiful. Right next to the table stood Emen. He was wearing a black suit with a red tie.

"You look beautiful" Emen told her as he she walked closer to him and the table.

"Are you kidding me. You look so handsome and I'm just wearing this. I should have dressed up more" Natasha told him nervously.

"I told you that you look beautiful. You don't need to change a single thing" emen told her and kissed her on the cheek. He pulled out her chair for her and she sat down. They had small talk through out the entire dinner. They didn't have to talk about anything important or special for the night to be amazing. They just had to be with each other. Soon dessert came and before she could even lift up her fork, he stopped her.

"Natasha. I know that this our first actual date, but you are my mate. You are the love of my life. I know we haven't even known each other that long either. None of this matters to me though. I just know and realize that after all of this, I couldn't lose you." Emen stood up and walked to her side of the table and got down on one of his knees and pulled out a ring box. He opened the box to show her an exquisite ring. "Please do me the honor of letting me love you forever. Will you, Natasha, Marry me" Emen asked her with hope in his eyes.

"Are you kidding me" Natasha asked him. She saw the glint of hope leave and she quickly put her hand on his shoulder as he went to stand up. "Of course I want to marry you" she whispered and squealed when he picked her up and spun her around.

"Well, that took long enough" a voice said off to the side. They both looked to see Bella standing beside a rose bush. "You told me that you'd ask the question fast" Bella complained.

"The question was actually quite fast in my opinion. I think it was the dinner that took forever" Emen stated in a teasing manner as Bella walked over towards them.

Natasha spun on Bella when Emen let her go. "Wait a minute. You knew about this" Natasha asked her.

"Of course. He asked me for permission to marry you about a week ago" Bella told her with a smirk.

"And you let me just wear this?" Natasha shrieked and jumped to tackle her sister, but Emen caught her. They all ended up on the ground wrestling until they grew so tired they just laid in the grass together. Laughing. Smiling. Together.

~~~Natasha's Thoughts~~~

To find your mate is one of the most amazing feelings in the world. You never grow tired of being around them. In fact, you always want to be around them. They just want to do everything in the world to make you happy. When you go through so much with your mate, it really only makes your relationship stronger than ever. I'm sure that no one has ever gone through as much as Emen and I have gone through in the past couple of months. We met under the most unfortunate circumstances. We fell for each other. I got pushed off of a train by a psychotic elderly man. My mother sold my little sister to the very same psychotic man who had pushed me off of the train. We had to go save my sister by me taking her place as his bride. I got stabbed and almost died. Then Emen proposed to me. Now
~~~

I'm here. I have a fiancée and my little sister together with me. I don't have to worry about her being with my mother because she will never have her. Speaking of which. My mother was sentenced to the death penalty and killed by the king. I didn't really want her dead, but I guess now we don't have to worry about her anymore. I'm so excited to get married and I can't wait to spend the rest of my life with the two most important people in my life. When it comes down to it, I'm glad that I went through all that I did. Every bad thing that happened made me who I am today and it gave me possession of my little sister and I found my mate. This has been such an adventure. I can only hope there will be more in the future. I'm sure there will be.

-games-fight-or-flight